Praise for Donald Lystra's
Season of Water and Ice

"Rich and wise and beautifully written…this novel again and again reminded me of why I fell in love with writing…the sudden but hard-won insights seem intensely real and right."—ELLEN AKINS, *Minneapolis Star Tribune*

"Lystra's graceful prose is evocative of place and time….This is a rich and satisfying read."—DONNA MARCHETTI, *The Cleveland Plain Dealer*

"The north woods of Michigan in 1957 proves rich emotional ground for Lystra's quietly impressive debut novel."—CHRISTOPHER POTTER, *Detroit Free Press*

"There's a transcendency (in the book) common to all good coming-of-age novels."—*Time Out Chicago* magazine

"Lystra…has written a beautiful novel that blends artistry with coming-of-age emotion."—ANN BYLE, *Grand Rapids Press*

Advance Praise for
Something that Feels like Truth

"In these stories, Donald Lystra explores with intelligence and empathy those moments, often very quiet, when people make the decisions that will change their lives. The prose is clean and crisp, allowing the emotional punch of each story to come unexpectedly, even long after the reading. I can't recommend *Something that Feels like Truth* highly enough."—KEITH TAYLOR, University of Michigan writing faculty; author of fourteen collections of poetry and short fiction

"Lystra's stories are marvelous vehicles of plainspoken power. Hop on, and you'll be astounded at where the short ride takes you."—LARRY WATSON, author of *Montana 1948* and *American Boy*

"What a pleasure to read these Carveresque stories of Michigan men. Lystra has a bead on working guys who haven't quite got a bead on their own lives, marriages, or dreams. These family men hunt and fish, work in auto plants or sell appliances, spend time alone in their basements, and occasionally tell a dirty joke to a pretty stranger at the Firefly Lounge. They yearn for something more without knowing what that something might be. Lystra's observations are keen and sometimes extravagant: when one character tips his La-Z-Boy all the way back, he is 'in the position of an astronaut in a space capsule;' a newly divorced man is 'learning to live with the sensation familiar to Arctic explorers and Michigan ice fishermen, of being supported by a fragile membrane, camped out on a crust of ice above a cold black void.' The beauty of these stories and their landscapes—physical and emotional—will surprise you."—BONNIE JO CAMPBELL, author of *Once Upon a River* and *American Salvage*

"Reader, you hold in your hand stories from the beating heart of America's hardscrabble core. Here at the edge of a lake, in rustling fields or raw pine scrub, and inside the worn beauty of small towns, Donald Lystra contemplates truth, family, character (or lack thereof), and what it means to be awake and alive. In plainspoken language Lystra reveals both the outward resourcefulness and the hidden tenderness of the Midwest. The people who live in these stories always turn and face their circumstances, sometimes early, sometimes at the final moment, but face them they do. Bringing us, breathless, alongside. Lystra is a precise and merciless writer, a master of that moment when life changes, often irreversibly."
—MARDI LINK, author *of Isadora's Secret* and *Hardscrabble*

"*Something that Feels like Truth* is as quiet and luminous as the cold night sky over Michigan. At the core of these elegant, unforgettable stories is a stillness that's mesmerizing. Like the great Midwestern writers Ernest Hemingway and William Maxwell, Lystra knows that riveting drama can be found in small moments, hidden behind the ordinary-looking doors of our neighbors. These are love stories, for the most part, about what happens when good people lose their passions and life leaves them stunned but not broken. Lystra is a writer of great wisdom and artistry, with a voice that makes you lean close and listen hard, shushing the noise around you so you will not miss a word.—VALERIE LAKEN, author of *Dream House* and *Separate Kingdoms*

"(Lystra) takes care in rendering the subtle, intimate moment, without rushing it or spinning it toward easier or artsier territory. He respects the complexity of real human interaction in fleeting moments. This is rare these days and reminds me of Richard Bausch, Richard Ford, and Ron Carlson."—STEVE AMICK, author of *The Lake, the River & the Other Lake* and *Nothing But a Smile*

Something that Feels like Truth

Also by Donald Lystra

SEASON *of* WATER *and* ICE

Something that Feels like Truth

Stories by Donald Lystra

SWITCHGRASS BOOKS *NIU Press DeKalb, Il*

© 2013 by Donald Lystra

Published by the Northern Illinois University Press, DeKalb, Illinois   60115

Manufactured in the United States using acid-free paper.

All Rights Reserved

Design by Yuni Dorr

Library of Congress Cataloging-in-Publication Data

Lystra, Donald.

Something that feels like truth : stories / Donald Lystra.

pages cm

ISBN 978-0-87580-693-8 (paperback : acid-free paper)

— ISBN 978-1-60909-089-0 (e-book)

I. Title.

PS3612.Y74S66 2013

813'.6—dc23

2013012982

This book is for Doni.

"All there is to thinking is seeing something noticeable, which makes you see something that you weren't noticing, which makes you see something that isn't even visible."

—**Norman Maclean**, *A River Runs Through It*

Contents

Introduction and Acknowledgments

When someone begins to write fiction late in life there is always the question of Why? When that someone has made his livelihood in a technical field like engineering, the question may be more emphatic because the presumption is that different and possibly incompatible skills are called for.

I wish I had a wise or interesting answer to the question of Why? but I'm afraid I don't; no better probably than a writer of any age or profession might offer. I always liked language and literature, but that is hardly unique. And I always had the feeling that I would *try* to write some day, when circumstances permitted. And I never believed in the left-brain/right-brain model of intelligence, so I wasn't daunted by the prejudgment that I couldn't do it, when the right time came.

And there is this, too: I've always believed that insights drawn from stark reality are of limited value when it comes to the most important questions of life. Fundamental truth—about love and purpose and character—always seemed to me as if it must derive from some blend of fact and imagination (or "thinking and dreaming" to use the words of Marilynne Robinson). So I may have simply wanted to venture into the murky territory of fundamental truth—while I still had my wits and energy—and the writing of fiction seemed the best way for me to go there.

That being said, I should add that I really don't know if the stories in this collection will bring readers closer to anything that can properly be thought of as truth. They *seemed* to do so for me, the writer of them, though I couldn't tell you exactly what the truth was that they revealed—only that each story seemed to settle some question or vague anxiety and to leave a kind of calmness behind. In that sense I may have learned that real truth is inexpressible, but only can be felt.

To the extent these stories succeed in capturing truth, or anything else of value, it's due to the help of very many people, and I want to thank them here. Josh Henkin, a wonderful writer and teacher of writing, led a number of workshops in which I participated, and effectively rescued me from the dead end I had wandered into on my own. John Dalton, the other professional writing teacher I've had the good luck to cross paths with, helped me immeasurably during a five-day summer workshop out in Iowa, and in many ways since. My early workshop partners, Nick Arvin, Mary Jean Babic, Valerie Laken, Leslie Stainton, Ami Walsh, Malina Williams, and my later workshop partners, Marty Calvert, Janet Gilsdorf, Jane Johnson, Danielle Lavaque-Manty, Margaret Nesse, Eleanor Shelton, have been great sources of help and inspiration. I'm fortunate and honored to count all of these people as friends.

Great thanks are also due to friends Pamela Grath and Tim Bazzett, who read an early version of the manuscript and provided valuable advice.

I wish to express my appreciation to the National Endowment for the Arts and to the MacDowell Colony for granting me fellowships which were important sources of support and encouragement.

Finally, I am grateful to the following publications in which these stories originally appeared:

"Bypass" (published as "We're All Adults") — *North American Review* (Jan./Feb. 2005)

"Family Way" — *Cimarron Review* (Fall 2006)

"Geese" — *Cottonwood* (Fall 2003)

"Hesitation" — *Other Voices* (Fall/Winter 2005)

"Infinite" (published as "Where Lou Gehrig Went After Leaving the Game") — *Green Mountains Review* (Vol. XVII, No. 1, 2004)

"Parallel Universe" — *The Greensboro Review* (Spring 2000)

"Rain Check" — *Meridian* (Fall/Winter 2001)

"Reckless" (published as "Rabbit Hunt") — *Southern Indiana Review* (Fall 2002)

"Speaking of Love Abstractly" (published as "The Tutor") — *The North American Review* (Nov./Dec. 2000)

"Treasure Hunt" (published as "Brother") — *Passages North* (Spring 2004)

Stories

Geese

We were sitting around Carl's big kitchen table—Carl, my wife Eileen, and me—waiting for the sun to come up over the frozen lake and for it to be time to take Carl into Muskegon for his cancer surgery. Eileen and I had driven up from Battle Creek the night before to be with Carl on his big day. Carl is a bachelor and lives alone.

Most of the conversation was happening between Carl and Eileen. I was doing my best to stay out of it, just studying our reflections in the big picture window that looked out over the lake—three bleary-eyed people in their bathrobes having coffee—and listening to the Canada geese that had gathered in front of Carl's.

"I don't want to talk about it any more," Eileen said, after a long silence had transpired. She was referring to Carl's sick dog, Buster, and whether to turn him over to the vets so he could be put out of his misery. The night before he'd kept us awake with his whimpering and his frightened little barks. Carl thought the time had come to face hard facts. "As far as I'm concerned the subject is closed," Eileen added. "It's just not going to happen." Her hand reached out and sliced the air.

"Well, it's a fact to be dealt with," Carl said. He blew on his coffee, sending a cloud of steam out to the center of the table. I watched it in the window, twisting in the air like a tortured phantom. "Besides, Buster's my dog if you recall."

"It'd be a terrible thing to do on this of all days," Eileen said.

"I'd hate to spoil the day for you."

"That's not what I meant, Carl."

"Maybe you'd like to go shopping instead. You could get yourself a dress, probably."

"Don't, Carl."

"You could get a nice dress for the funeral."

Eileen folded her arms and stared hard at the floor. Lately, Carl was acting as if his cancer gave him the right to say anything he pleased. Most of what was driving him was fear, though. The doctors called it exploratory surgery, but Carl expected the worst.

A few seconds passed in awkward silence. I watched in the window as the defiance slowly drained from Carl's expression. This did not surprise me. Carl is not a person who can hold a strong emotion for very long.

"Maybe I'll call and put off the surgery," he announced in a thoughtful voice, as if the idea had just occurred to him. He scrunched his face and stared off like he was weighing the pros and cons of some important matter— whether there's such a thing as original sin, or if the polar ice cap is melting. "I could take Buster to the vets today and they could reschedule the operation for later."

Eileen reached across and placed her hand on Carl's arm. "That's probably not a good idea, honey," she said, and I knew exactly what she was thinking. These days Carl couldn't take five steps without running out of breath. Later for Carl was now.

I pushed up out of my chair and went over to the picture window. What to do with sick dogs and sick people were not subjects high on my agenda on this day or any other. I just wanted Carl's operation to be over so Eileen and I could get back to our normal life in Battle Creek.

"What do you think, Glenn?" Eileen asked, turning in my direction.

I made a tunnel with my hands and pressed my face up to the cool pane of glass. Outside, bare branches showed black against a pink horizon. A white sheet of ice covered the lake except in front of Carl's where an underground spring fed out warm water. Scores of geese had gathered there on the open water, more than I had ever seen. A couple of swans, too.

"Glenn and me are here because we love you, Carl,"

Eileen said, after a moment had passed. "Isn't that so, Glenn?"

Outside, two geese came in for a landing. They came down slowly, their spindly legs thrust forward, wings cupped and flexing against the rush of cold December air. They settled onto the glassy surface with barely a splash.

Eileen and Carl were closer than most brothers and sisters, and that was something I had learned to live with. When they were just kids their mother had run off to Oregon with a man who raised hunting dogs, and she had not come back, and so Eileen—who was nine years older than Carl—had become a sort of substitute mother. She saw that Carl got decent meals and clothes, and made sure he stayed in line at school. You could almost say that Eileen had made a career out of Carl, getting him out of scrapes and talking sense into him when his fiery emotions threatened to carry him away. Most people who knew Carl gave him a wide berth, but Eileen saw qualities in him that others didn't. She said that Carl was cursed with an intelligence that made him react to things more powerfully. More than once I've awakened in the middle of the night and found her downstairs at the kitchen table, the telephone up to her ear, talking to Carl in that soft, measured voice of hers, that sweet, middle-of-the-night voice that held the promise that, come morning, everything would be all right.

Eileen and I had met at the community college in '68. She was studying textile design and had the intention of going to New York to strike it big in the fashion industry. I was taking night classes in car mechanics, which was the professional field I had chosen to pursue, and did. But right from the start it was clear to me that Eileen was deceiving herself about the fashion industry. The problem wasn't that she didn't have talent—she had plenty, even I could see it—but with Carl in the picture she wasn't likely to be venturing very far from Battle Creek. Still, I was impressed that she held onto that hope and plowed ahead against obstacles that would have daunted a lesser spirit. Lives are built on dreams, after all, and that has to be respected.

As for me and Carl, we got along in a kind of manly, grudging way. Outside of Eileen, we had few things in common. Carl liked to hunt while I tend toward gentler pursuits—golf and bowling is what I enjoy—but we always managed to find a few subjects to talk about when we were thrown together. In my opinion, Carl could never accept the fact that Eileen had chosen to take a husband, and all that that implied. On my side, I saw Carl as part of the package—good and bad—that comes with someone that you marry.

It was six o'clock now, and I was anxious for the day to start and for it to fill up with some distractions. Almost anything would do besides sick dogs and people. I left Carl and Eileen in the kitchen and wandered into the utility room to check on Buster. I found him lying on an old quilt next to the clothes dryer, a big black Labrador that had seen better days. He lifted his head and watched me with eyes that had no spark of interest.

I knelt down and began rubbing Buster's ears. He settled his head back onto the quilt, closed his eyes and emitted a dull, mournful sigh. For a while, just to kill time, I pretended I was a holy man who could put vital energy back into Buster's wasted body. It was like a TV show I had seen about a man who had special powers. I put my hand on Buster's head and closed my eyes and tried to make my mind go blank. I guess that's what I thought it would feel like if you had special powers.

I was startled back to reality by Carl's voice coming from right behind me.

"What do you think, Glenn?" he asked.

It took me a moment to collect myself. "About what?" I said.

"About Buster. That's the topic of the hour, isn't it?"

I kept my hand on Buster's head, working my fingers through his limp fur. "You probably shouldn't decide anything too fast, Carl."

"Me and Buster are quite a pair, aren't we?" Carl said, and I noticed that his voice was louder than it needed to be. "Maybe you should take us both to the vets. They could do two for the price of one."

"Don't talk like that, Carl," I said. "That's not a healthy

way to talk. You know the operation's going to turn out fine."

"Is that so?" he said, still loud. "Well, thanks for that information, Glenn. I guess that settles everything, then, doesn't it?"

I didn't know what to say and so I didn't say anything. But I didn't like the way Carl was acting. He seemed to be working himself into one of his agitated states.

I stood up so I could see Carl better. Carl is a big man with hair that has gone mostly gray. He has small, sensitive eyes that remind you of a woman. When he gets excited he looks at people in quick, sideways glances. That's how he was looking at me now.

"Maybe I could take Buster to the vets for you," I said. I was trying to think of something that would calm Carl down, plus give me something to stay occupied.

"No," Carl said. "I should handle it myself, Glenn. Buster's my dog and I should handle it."

"Ordinarily, maybe, but not today. Today is different, Carl. Today you want your mind to be relaxed, just like Eileen says."

Carl stared at me like a man caught in a bad dream. Then his gaze traveled across the room and fixed on something.

"The way I'm thinking won't take that much time," he said.

I turned around to see what Carl was looking at. And I saw it was his gun cabinet in the corner.

"Carl," I said, "if it's going to be done you want to have it done professionally. Turn Buster over to the vet.

That's the way to handle it."

"Buster deserves better than to be pumped full of chemicals by a bunch of strangers," he said. His voice had a raspy edge that made it sound strange and crazy. He blinked his eyes and looked at me in that sideways way.

"That's not the point," I said, and I noticed that my own voice was loud now, too. "Doing it yourself is a bad idea with you going in for surgery."

Carl stepped in front of me as if to show that the subject was closed, as far as he was concerned. He opened the gun cabinet and took a pistol off the shelf. I recognized it as one I'd seen him use to shoot a snapping turtle on a stump. That was probably ten years ago.

"Carl," I said. "We should think about this."

"What's going on?" It was Eileen's voice. She was standing in the doorway.

"Carl wants to take care of Buster himself," I said. "He wants to handle it in a personal way."

Eileen took a hurried step into the room. When she saw the pistol in Carl's hand a kind of shudder went though her body. She stared at the gleaming metal in startled disbelief. And I could sense a battle beginning to rage inside of her, between her normal sweetness and something else. And who could blame her? She'd been working all morning to keep Carl in the right frame of mind to have his operation. Now everything was slipping away in a single wild moment.

"Are you crazy, Carl?" she said. "Do you want to saturate your mind with thoughts of death today, you who's already so afraid." The words tumbled out of Eileen's mouth. And I knew they were the wrong ones.

Carl gave Eileen a long reproachful stare. Then he slid the pistol out of the holster and turned it slowly in his hand, as if he was examining it for some mechanical defect. Then he placed his free hand against the wall and began to lower himself to the floor, using the slow deliberate movements of a person much older than he was.

For one extravagant moment I thought Carl meant to shoot Buster right there on the floor. I looked over at Eileen, expecting her to take control of things like she always did. But I could tell from her face that she had no answer for this particular madness.

"Carl!" I said. I knelt down and put my hand over his that held the gun.

Carl turned to me, his face swollen with the emotions of a man who doesn't know where life is taking him, or whether it will bring him back. I tightened my grip and pushed against his shoulder, trying to keep the gun barrel pointed at the floor. In spite of his frailness, Carl kept twisting and throwing me off balance. Then he gave a sudden lurch and I felt his hand begin to slip free from my grip.

Behind us, Eileen was making sounds like a frightened animal. Her normal calm demeanor had finally been overthrown. I thought to myself that this was how things happened that you read about in newspapers, terrible things that you believed would never touch you or become part of your life. Then I tried to think of what I could say to make the crazy moment end, and there was only one thing I could think of, and so I said it.

"I'll do it!" As soon as the words were out, Carl's hand went slack. I lifted the gun away and stood up and turned toward Eileen.

"Nobody's doin' anything," she said. "Buster'll stay here and we'll all go to the hospital together. Just like we planned."

I looked back and forth between Eileen and Carl, not knowing what I should do next. Carl was still kneeling on the floor, but a little of the wildness had left his face. It'd been replaced with something calmer, something I took to be relief.

"No," I said, turning back to Eileen. "It's important to Carl. You two leave for the hospital. I'll take care of Buster and catch up with you after. That's the way we should do it, sweetheart. Then everybody's happy."

Eileen stared at me as if I was a traitor or had lost my mind. When it came to Carl, she wasn't used to being overruled.

"You've never even used a gun, Glenn," she said, as if that was a terrible shortcoming.

"I've seen Carl do it, honey. I saw him shoot a turtle once."

Our gazes came together, Eileen's and mine, and I could feel the anger stretched tight in her. It's not often we disagree but this time was different; this time I remembered the look on Carl's face and held my ground.

A moment passed. Eileen turned and left the room.

❋   ❋   ❋

I went back to the kitchen to have another cup of coffee while Carl and Eileen got ready to leave for the hospital. I was upset by the promise I'd made to Carl. I had never killed a living thing before, or ever wanted to, and now I was committed to shooting poor old Buster. I sat and sipped my coffee and tried not to think about it.

After a few minutes, Eileen came out. She was wearing a gray skirt and a sweater with an unusual pattern that bespoke her background in textiles. She went over to the window and began to comb her hair in the reflection.

"Did you ever see so many geese?" I said to her.

She kept combing her hair.

"It's because Carl's got the only open water on the lake. Geese need open water to swim in. Otherwise they head south."

Eileen finished with her hair and turned around and fixed me with a level stare. "Now let me get this straight," she said. "Carl and I are going to leave for the hospital so he can have his cancer operation, and you're going to stay behind and shoot his dog. Is that the plan?"

I didn't say anything. I could tell it was a question that didn't need an answer.

"Did you think about what this is going to do to Carl?" Eileen asked. "He loves that dog."

"I'm just trying to do the right thing, sweetheart," I said. "It'll ease Carl's mind to know Buster is being taken care of by family." I stepped forward to touch Eileen's arm but she made a motion with her hands and backed away. "I'm just trying to do what's best for Carl," I said again, which was the only thing I was really sure about.

Eileen went back to get her coat and then Carl came out. He had on a gray suit that hung loosely on his shrunken frame and a wide colorful tie from about twenty-five years ago. The thought of Carl getting dressed up to go to the hospital struck me as funny, but I didn't say anything. I knew he'd been back saying good-bye to Buster.

"Here," he said. He passed the pistol over to me. "I've put a magazine in it." He touched a tiny red button just behind the trigger. "That right there is the safety."

I hefted the gun. It felt solid and powerful. I sighted down the barrel at a coffee cup sitting on the counter. Then I laid it on the table.

Just then Eileen came back wearing her blue ski parka. I hugged her but she stiffened and pulled away. I shook Carl's hand and then they both went out through the side door. Carl stood on the stoop while Eileen backed the Bronco around, then Carl went down the steps and got in on the passenger's side. In the glare of the headlights tiny snowflakes drifted down, just wispy pieces of ice floating in the frigid air. I stood and watched the red taillights bump out of sight down Carl's two-track road.

It felt good to be alone and to be able to forget about Carl for a while. I sat in an easy chair and looked through one of Carl's *Field and Streams*. Then I watched *Good Morning America* on TV. Diane Sawyer talked to a scientist about global warming and then a man came on with dancing parrots. Then it was nine o'clock and I decided I had better get moving.

While I was getting dressed I thought about what I had to do. There was a stand of pine trees in the woods behind Carl's house and I decided that would be a good place to do it. I knew Buster was too lame to walk that far, but I thought I could drag him over the ground on the quilt, or use a wheelbarrow. Then other questions started crowding into my head, practical questions I hadn't thought about, like where, exactly, I should aim the pistol and what I should do with Buster afterwards.

I began to feel strange. My thoughts were darting around like ants when a rock has been turned over. I began to wonder if there was another way to do it, maybe take Buster to the vets without telling anyone, or feed him a handful of Carl's pills so he'd just slip away peacefully. I was beginning to understand there's more to shooting something than I had realized and I wasn't sure I could pull it off. I pictured Carl and Eileen out on the road in Carl's Bronco and suddenly I wished I was with them and not where I was.

Finally, I managed to pull myself together. I stuffed Carl's pistol into my pocket and lifted Buster up from the utility room floor, quilt and all, and carried him back to the spot that I had been thinking about. Then I offered up a little prayer and then I picked up the gun.

It was over so fast I almost didn't realize what had happened. All it took was a little squeeze and the pistol jumped in my hand and Buster slumped into the snow like a puppet with the strings cut. The sound of the gun left a big impression on me though, the explosion going out into the forest and then the echo crashing back and back and back, and then hearing the cry and flutter of a startled flock of crows, and then everything getting quiet again and peaceful and like before, except Buster was dead.

I went back to the house and got a shovel. My hands were shaking so badly I could barely hold it. The ground was frozen but I was able to bust through the top layer and get into the soft earth where it was easier digging. I dug like a madman and made a nice deep hole, then I wrapped Buster in the quilt and lifted him down. I tried not to look as I filled the hole, first with the soft earth and then with the frozen clods. The last thing I did was to roll a big white stone on top, because I wanted to be able to find the spot later, and show Carl, if I had the chance.

I stood up and looked around. A north wind had come up that was driving the snowflakes slantwise with the ground. The wind and the slanted snow made everything white and furious and off-balance, and for a minute I wondered if I would be able to find my way back to the house. My heart was pounding and the cold wind was blowing on my face.

I had kept my promise to Carl but I didn't feel good about it. Buster was lying dead in a hole and I was the undisputed cause of it. I tried to remind myself it was the worn-out Buster I had shot, but my mind kept seeing the young Buster fetching sticks and swimming in the lake. That was the hardest part: knowing that *that* Buster was gone now, too, and everything connected to him.

I stepped over to where I had buried Buster. "Please accept this fine dog into your kingdom," I blurted out, which was something I remembered seeing in a movie. Then I turned and hurried back to the house.

When I got to the house the phone was ringing. It was Eileen at the hospital.

"They just took Carl back into the operating room," she said, in a cool voice. "I thought you might like to know that. I'm here in the lobby."

Before I could say anything there was a muffled sound as if Eileen had taken the receiver away from her ear. I heard her talking to someone in the background, then she came back on the line. "Listen, Glenn, there's a lot of people here so I can't talk for long. It's like Grand Central Station. Everybody's relative is getting operated on today, I guess."

"How was Carl when he went in?" I asked.

"Fine," she said. "Kind of stunned. Just doing whatever the nurses told him to do. Go here. Go there."

For a while we didn't say anything. I still had that strange feeling from being back in the woods and my heart was pounding like crazy. I moved over to the picture window and looked out onto the lake. The Canada geese were still down there, only now the north wind was riffling the water and a black skin of ice was starting to form. The geese paddled and flapped their wings, trying to keep some open water around them. At Eileen's end I heard a door slam.

"He cried a little on the drive in," Eileen said. "Not bad, though. He just started talking about Mom and Dad and then he broke down for a minute."

"I guess that's to be expected."

"I suppose."

"Eileen," I said. "I took care of that business with Buster."

"Oh," she said, cool.

"I was hoping I could let Carl know before he went in for his operation. So his mind would be settled about it." Out on the lake, the geese were bobbing and weaving, working to keep the water free. "Maybe you can tell him when he comes out."

There was another long silence. It lasted so long I began to think we'd been cut off. But finally Eileen's voice came back. "Listen, Glenn," she said, "I'm tired of talking about that damn dog. As far as I'm concerned it was a needless aggravation."

"To you," I said, "and to me. But maybe not to Carl."

Eileen went silent again. And I knew she was thinking about what I had just said, and what she would say back. In the eerie silence coming over the wire I could faintly hear her breathing. The whispery sound of it, that slight rush of air, seemed like the only connection I had to things right then. To Eileen or to anyone.

I stood completely still, holding the receiver, waiting for Eileen to answer. And I thought about Carl stretched out on a table in a room with blazing lights, and how that was the right place for him to be, and how Eileen and I had gotten him there in spite of everything that had worked against us. And then I thought about how I'd stepped up when Eileen had been pushed too far, and the risk I'd run by shooting Buster. And then I thought about going home to Battle Creek, where Eileen and I could resume our normal happy life together. Nothing about today seemed normal, nothing at all.

I counted five of Eileen's breaths.

"Just get yourself in here, sweetheart," she said to me at last. "I guess I see your point. We'll call a truce."

I held the phone up tight against my ear. Out on the lake, a goose pulled himself up onto the skin of ice but it broke and he fell back into the water, flapping his wings.

"Eileen," I said.

"What?"

I heard her breathing on the wire. My heart was going like crazy.

"Don't hang up yet."

Reckless

We drove up from Detroit and spent the night at the Chippewa Hotel in Grayling, an old-fashioned drummers' hotel whose broad front porch held an assortment of rust-spotted lawn chairs. In the morning we ate pancakes in the hotel dining room beneath murals of whitetail deer jumping over fallen logs, Canada geese on the wing, beavers constructing a dam. My father talked about his friend, Joe Gallager, who we were meeting that morning to go rabbit hunting with. He had known him from the old days, back when he—my father—was learning the tool-and-die trade at a General Motors factory in Grand

Rapids. Gallager had been a millwright, he said, one of the workers who set the chains onto the large steel stamping dies so they could be lifted by cranes and moved around the factory. I remember thinking that it seemed like an unusual career, not a thing that would occupy a man for a lifetime, but my father explained that the steel dies that shaped the car body panels could be as big as a room. Knowing how to rig them so they could be lifted and moved overhead above the assembly lines—how to do that without endangering yourself or the men working down below—took considerable skill.

My father drained the last of his coffee, then he looked around the nearly empty dining room as if he half-expected to see someone he recognized. "You'll get a kick out of watching Gallager's hounds work," he said. "Once they lock onto a scent there's no stopping them. They'll follow a rabbit to hell and back if they have to." And he laughed in a way I hadn't heard him laugh for a long time, sort of careless and relaxed and indifferent to the consequences.

My father loved the outdoor life. That's one sure thing you could say about him. He could tell you when caddis flies were hatching on a trout stream, or how to bring down a deer with a single rifle shot, or where pheasant could be found in a field of corn. He had learned these things growing up in western Michigan during the Depression, when hunting and fishing were reasonable ways of putting food onto the family table, and he had continued to love that life as an adult. Most weekends found him in the woods or fields with his friends, men like him who worked in a factory and longed for a diversion, some taste of freedom, on their days off.

But in 1959—when the things happened that I am going to tell you about—my father received a promotion that took him to the company's central offices in Detroit. He was a large man with strong large hands and the ability to look at situations and understand them. And he had always been a hard worker, wanting to make a success of his life and leave behind the poverty he had known as a boy. But the suburban community where he brought my mother and me was different from the factory towns we'd lived in before; in this world of gently curving streets and lushly tended landscapes it was hard for him to practice his old pursuits; and it wasn't just the lack of open spaces, lakes and streams and forests; it was something else: a change in what was expected of him by the company, maybe, or what he expected of himself, now that he was in the management ranks. His new colleagues in the central offices were careful, disciplined men—accountants and lawyers and engineers—who spent their weekends golfing or playing tennis or sailing yachts on Lake St. Clair. The hunting and fishing that my father had grown up doing, and that he loved to do, were not popular with these men.

It was hard for me to know how all of this affected him, or what other things were happening that I was not aware of, but there were signs that his life had changed in ways he did not completely like. I remember waking in the night in our big new house and hearing hushed, urgent-sounding conversations coming from my parents' bedroom down the hall. And I remember watching my father in the evening as he sat in his big leather chair, smoking cigarettes and staring off into space, oblivious to the television set crackling in the corner.

One autumn evening after a sudden rainstorm I spotted him from my upstairs bedroom window, practicing fly-fishing casts in the back yard. Still wearing his crisp white shirt from work, he built huge figure-eights with his fly line in the sodden September air, dropping his 9-foot tapered leader at the edges of my mother's flower beds, delicate as a breath. Again and again the line floated down and came to rest against the shiny blades of grass, and each time he allowed it to rest there for a moment, an expectant look on his face, as if he actually believed he might coax a trout out from under the begonias. Finally, he reeled in the line and broke the bamboo rod down into sections, and slipped them one by one into the aluminum carrying case. But he continued to stand there, staring through the darkening twilight of our new neighborhood, until all I could see was the bright smudge of his white shirt. And I remember wondering what he must be thinking, a man in a white dress shirt with a fly rod in his hand, looking out across the perfectly manicured landscape of his new back yard, all lushly green, trimmed, and tended, conforming perfectly with the obligations of his new constricted life.

❄   ❄   ❄

Gallager lived in a small wood-framed house that sat back from a gravel road, surrounded by stacks of firewood and pieces of rusted farm machinery. You reached the house by a two-track drive that meandered through a stand of poplars. As we drove up that December morning, I remember thinking that someone had probably followed that path the first time they had driven onto the property and then had just kept on using it out of habit. It wasn't a thing that had been planned, in other words, but just something that had happened for no good reason.

My father tapped twice on the horn and after a few minutes Gallager came out, a small, grizzled man, older than my father, who walked in a stiff, straight-legged way. He came toward us with his hand outstretched, and right away I noticed the odd shape of it, the two smallest fingers missing and a section of the palm gone, too.

"Hell, Tom, it's good to see you," Gallager said, shaking my father's hand.

"This is Jamie," my father said, putting a hand onto my shoulder. I hesitated for a second and then stepped forward and grasped Gallager's hand. I expected it to feel odd, perhaps even repulsive, but the only sensation was of its smallness, as if I were shaking the hand of a child.

"Are you a rabbit hunter?" Gallager asked me.

"I guess so," I said.

"Well, we're going to do some rabbit hunting today," he said, and he laughed in the same careless way my father had laughed in the hotel dining room, and my father laughed, too.

Gallager went back into the house and returned a moment later with a shotgun and a red plaid hunting jacket that he put into the back of a battered Ford pick-up. Then he went behind the house where I could hear the sounds of braying dogs and he came back carrying two beagles, one under each arm, like sacks of flour. The little dogs squirmed and pawed the air but it was obvious they weren't going to get free from Gallager's tight grip. It was a funny sight, though, a man carrying two dogs like that, something you didn't expect to see and that you'd never see in the suburbs, probably. Gallager hoisted the dogs over the side of the pick-up, one by one, and set them down, and immediately they began to rush back and forth in the truck bed, their claws scratching and clicking against the metal, sounding eager and furious.

My father went over to our car and got our shotguns out of the trunk. He set them in the truck bed next to Gallager's and then the three of us hoisted ourselves up into the cab, me in the middle. It was a tight fit, each of us bulky in our heavy wool hunting clothes, but it felt good to be setting off on a trip with two grown men and I was happy and feeling good about how the day was unfolding.

"I'm taking you out to a place I know about," Gallager said, backing the truck around.

"State land?" my father asked.

"No. It belongs to a fellow I know about."

"He won't mind us hunting there?" my father asked.

"I suppose not," Gallager said, and he smiled and winked at me.

We drove along the gravel roads. My father and Gallager talked about the days when they had worked together in the Fisher Body factory in Grand Rapids. They had known each other during the sit-down strike of '37, when the men had stopped working and refused to leave the factory, and they told stories about that time, laughing at things that had meaning to them but didn't mean anything to me. I enjoyed listening to their talk, though, because it was a kind of talk I expected to do some day, too.

"So now you've gone over to management," Gallagher said, and I knew he was referring to my father's recent promotion.

"I guess you could say that," my father said. "A man's got to try to rise in the world, Joe."

Gallager glanced in my direction. "Your Daddy's become an important man, Jamie," he said.

"Don't put the boy on the spot, Joe," my father said, and he gave a short embarrassed laugh.

"Well, he ought to be proud that his Daddy's risen in the world." Gallager said, though something about the way he spoke the words made me think he didn't truly mean them.

"Yes, sir," I said. "I am."

We drove along for a while in silence, past an abandoned farmhouse and a field of Christmas trees laid out in perfect rows; then Gallager noticed me staring at his hand. He grinned and held it up so I could get a better look. Along the cut-away edge the skin was white and mottled, like wax that has melted and run together, not really like skin at all. A raised flap ran around the old wound, like an ugly red welt.

"Do you like my mitt, Jamie?" he asked me.

"I guess it's all right," I said, although seeing it like that made me feel a little sick.

"It was my retirement present," Gallager said. "It got me a pension to move north on." And I smiled because it seemed like something that was meant to be funny.

We drove a ways further and then Gallager pulled off into a cherry orchard. The truck bounced along between the rows of trees, the leafless branches scraping the cab, sounding like the furious clawing of some large animal. Then we came out of the orchard into a large open field filled with charred tree stumps.

Gallager pulled the truck up to the edge of the burned-over field where a forest began and we all got out. He went back to the truck bed and my father walked over to the edge of the forest. "This land is posted," he said. He was looking at a bright red NO TRESPASSING sign that was nailed to a tree trunk.

"That don't matter, Tom," Gallager said. He dropped the tailgate and the dogs jumped down. Right away they struck a rigid posture, their noses raised and their nostrils flexing. They sniffed the air, ran a few steps, and then got quiet and rigid and sniffed again. It was something to see.

"I don't like hunting on posted land," my father said.

Gallager lifted the guns out of the truck bed. "It'll be

okay, Tom," he said. He handed one of the guns to my father. "I know the owner."

My father stared at Gallager as if he didn't believe what he was saying, but Gallager was already putting shells into the chamber of his shotgun. "You ever seen a beagle dog work, Jamie?" he asked.

"No, sir," I said.

"Well, it's a pretty sight," he said. And then he explained about how a rabbit will run in a circle when he is chased by dogs, and how, as a hunter, you set yourself up near where the rabbit was jumped and wait for him to circle back. "A rabbit lives on only an acre or two of land," Gallager said. "So he wants to come back to that same place. It's just his nature."

I thought about what Gallager said, and I was pleased to learn that unusual fact about rabbits. Although it saddened me, too, knowing that you could use their natural instincts to shoot them, and I thought it was a kind of low thing to do. But I didn't say anything because I knew it was just a thought that was my own thought and wouldn't mean anything to the men.

My father handed me a gun and we set off, the three of us arranged more or less in a line, following the edge of the woods where there were piles of brush and an old split-rail fence, places where a rabbit might hide. The hounds ranged out in front of us, sniffing the ground, nervous and excited. And Gallager had been right, because it was a pretty sight to see those dogs doing the thing they were meant to do more than anything else in the world. And

I thought to myself that I should pay close attention to everything that was happening, because I knew I would want to remember it later when I could think about it better.

We walked along for several minutes, following the edge of the woods, and then there was a sudden flash as a rabbit darted out from a brush pile, leaping away toward the woods with the dogs right behind, braying and howling.

"Take him, Tom!" Gallager shouted.

My father sighted his gun but he did not fire. He stood holding the gun in position against his cheek, watching the dogs disappear into the heavy brush.

"Why didn't you shoot him, Tom?" Gallager asked.

"I guess I'm a little nervous to be shooting in a crowd," my father said.

"Hell, Tom, me and Jamie don't care if we have to carve a few pellets out of our backsides. Do we, Jamie?"

"No, sir," I said, and I smiled, because it seemed like a joke that one man would tell to another.

My father didn't say anything; he just looked at Gallager and then at me. And I thought he was embarrassed to have missed his chance to shoot a rabbit, and I felt a sudden shame for having smiled at Gallager's joke.

Gallager turned to me. "You stand over there, Jamie," he said, pointing the barrel of his gun toward a grove of birch trees. "We'll let you have the next crack at him. When the rabbit comes back he'll run through right about there. I'm going to follow along behind my dogs and keep them moving."

Gallager started off into the woods and I walked over to the spot where he had said to stand. After a minute my father came over and stood beside me. "He'll be coming out of the tree line over there," he said, and he pointed at the same spot Gallager had just indicated to me. "Wait until you're sure you have a good shot."

We stood watching the opening where the rabbit would come through. I was excited, and I noticed that I was breathing hard. I had never shot a rabbit and I wondered how I would handle it. I tried to focus all of my attention onto the right spot so I would not make a mistake and waste my opportunity.

We stood quietly. The braying of the dogs grew fainter as they moved off into the woods. And then we couldn't hear them at all.

A few more minutes passed. I began to get restless. It seemed to me the dogs should have brought the rabbit back by now. But I didn't know that for sure and so I just stood there waiting. And then my attention began to wander, and I began to notice things I hadn't noticed before: the mottled gray sky with the sun a vague white ball behind it, little patterns of melting frost on the ground, the sound of dry leaves rustling in the breeze, the chirping of a sparrow.

My father walked over to the edge of the woods and peered through the trees. Then he came back. "I guess Gallager's dogs have gotten away from him," he said. He smiled in a bitter way and shook his head. Then he looked up to where another NO TRESPASSING sign was nailed

to a tree. "It's probably just as well. We're not even supposed to be hunting here."

He leaned his gun against a tree and lit a cigarette,
which surprised me, because smoking was something you
weren't supposed to do on a hunt. "Your Dad's showing
you how to poach game from somebody else's property,
Jamie," he said. He gave a snap of his wrist and the match
went out. "That'll be a good lesson for you to take back
home, won't it? Something to tell your new friends about."

We stood there, me holding the gun and my father
smoking his cigarette, and I could tell that something
about the day was changing for him: his estimation of
Gallager, but also his feelings about hunting, maybe, and
about himself. After a while I moved the shotgun back to
the crook of my arm where it felt less heavy.

"How did Gallager mangle his hand?" I asked, because
it was something I had been thinking about.

My father turned to me with a surprised expression, as
if he had to remind himself who I was and what I was
doing there. Then he took a drag on his cigarette and blew
a stream of smoke out into the air.

"I only heard about it later," he said. "He was steadying
a quarter-panel die that was being moved by a crane. And
he was acting funny, cutting up, like he did sometimes.
Maybe he was drunk. Who knows? Anyway, the crane
operator started to lower the die and it began to swing and
Gallager made a quick grab to steady it. But somehow his
two fingers slipped between the sections just as it touched
the floor." He took another drag on his cigarette and blew

out the smoke. "A man who saw it said it was all over in an instant. Gallager's fingers just sort of disappeared into the steel."

I tried to picture what my father was describing but it was hard because I didn't know what a die was, except that it was a large piece of machinery and was made of solid steel. But I understood how a man could be reckless for a moment and lose his fingers. And then I wondered how it felt when something like that happens—a part of you gets torn away—whether it comes as a terrible pain that you can barely stand, or if it is just a thing that happens and then you notice it. And I decided, then, that I would make a point of always being careful, and learn to pay attention to things, so that nothing like that would ever happen to me.

Just then I heard a sound. When I looked I saw Gallager walking toward us through the forest. He moved slowly, his shotgun cradled in the crook of his arm, stopping every few steps to take a leisurely look around.

"Where do you suppose those dogs have gone, Joe?" my father called out when Gallager was still some distance away.

Gallager waited until he had come closer before he answered. "It's hard to say, Tom," he said "Sometimes you can't control them."

"I thought they were trained."

"Training will only go so far, Tom. Sometimes they just get an idea in their head and take off on their own."

My father dropped his cigarette onto the ground and

stepped on it. "Well, whatever happened, it looks like they're not coming back. So I guess Jamie and I'll just make our own way back to the highway. Maybe we can kick up a few rabbits by accident."

"You don't have to do that, Tom. We can still hunt together."

My father looked at Gallager. His head was tilted back, as if he were examining something he did not completely understand, or perhaps did not want to. "We'll just make our own way back," he said again. "We can hitch a ride when we get to the highway." He walked over to his gun and picked it up. "Come on, Jamie," he said.

We'd gone a few steps in the direction of the forest when Gallager called out. "What about the dogs? Who's going to help me round them up?" He said it in a sharp way that made us stop and turn around.

"I guess I'll leave that in your hands, Joe," my father said.

Both men looked at each other for what seemed like a long time. Gallager's face was full of emotions, although I couldn't tell you exactly what they were: anger, probably, and maybe confusion. He was breathing hard and standing with his feet apart, and I thought that he wanted to fight my father, and I was surprised at how relaxed my father looked, because I had never seen him fight a man and I didn't know if he knew how.

"Calm down, Joe," my father said. "Jamie doesn't need to see two grown men going at each other."

For a minute nothing happened. It was just the three of

us standing in the woods alone. I heard the wind moving through the treetops, the rustling of leaves, the chittering of a squirrel. And then all of a sudden something seemed to change because my father took a couple of steps in Gallager's direction, just easy and casual steps, everyday like. "You think you'll be able to round up your dogs, Joe?" he said, and he spoke in a gentle voice, as if he were talking across the back fence to a neighbor.

Gallager didn't say anything, but his gaze shifted away from my father's face.

"Well, then, Jamie and I'll just head along, if that's all right."

"You can do what you want," Gallager said. He turned and spit onto the ground.

For a moment my father kept looking at Gallager, and then he did something that surprised me: he reached out and touched Gallager's arm just above the elbow. It was a gesture I'd seen him use before, with my mother, to help her down a step or guide her through an open door. He held Gallager's arm like that for just a moment and then he turned away and walked off into the field of charred stumps. And this time I knew he was not coming back and so I followed along behind, running a little to catch up.

We walked a long way and finally came to a road where my father flagged down a car that gave us a ride back to Gallager's house. As he was laying our shotguns in the trunk of the car I asked him where we were going to hunt next.

"Maybe we'll just call it a day," he said. "Would that break your heart?"

I said that I still wanted to hunt, because it was still early and I did.

My father slammed down the trunk. The sound of it echoed back in the trees. "Without dogs it'd just be a hit and miss affair, Jamie," he said. "That's where Gallager let us down."

"Why didn't we stay and help him find his dogs?"

My father looked at me. "I guess your father just had a change of heart," he said.

We got into the car and retraced our path down Gallager's winding two-track drive and out onto the dirt road.

"I suppose you think your Dad's crazy," my father said, after we'd driven a few miles in silence. He reached across and felt blindly in the glove box for a pack of cigarettes. Then he punched the lighter on the dashboard. "Or maybe a traitor. One or the other."

"No," I said. I *had* been thinking those things but I didn't want to say it.

The lighter popped out and my father took it and touched it to the end of his cigarette, which flared red against his face. "Men like Gallager," he said, talking around the cigarette, "they live away from people and think they don't have to answer for anything. But that's not true. There are certain rules, whether you live up north or anywhere else." He blew a stream of smoke against the windshield where it flattened and spread. "You understand what I'm saying, Jamie?"

I was looking out the side window. We were passing through a cedar swamp with oily-looking water standing in ditches alongside the road. I knew my father was waiting for an answer but I didn't want to speak. I still didn't understand why he had gotten mad at Gallager, who had only been guilty of losing his dogs as far as I could tell, or why he'd decided that we couldn't hunt any more.

"It's something good for you to learn," my father said, after another moment had passed. "It'll mean something to you one day."

Still I did not say anything because I didn't believe what he was saying and didn't want to lie. He was just speaking words for my consumption, that's what I believed, words he felt he had to say to make sense of a situation.

We drove along in silence; then we came into the town of Grayling.

"I like Gallager," my father said suddenly, as if there had been no interruption to our conversation. Up ahead the Chippewa Hotel loomed into view with its broad front porch and rows of empty chairs facing onto the street. "But he's a careless man, Jamie. Reckless, I'd say. Not a good influence."

I looked over at my father. He was staring ahead through the windshield, his brow furrowed, like a man working through some difficult problem in mathematics. And then he felt my stare and turned and half-smiled at me. And even though he had been the cause of it—had brought it on himself and for no good reason—I knew he felt bad about how the day had turned out: that we hadn't seen the beagles work or shot a single rabbit. And I felt perhaps he was also wondering when we would get another chance to do those things, or if we would ever do them again.

"I want us to have a good life, Jamie," he said, speaking with more force than was his custom. "That's not such a bad thing, is it?"

I turned my head and watched through the mud-streaked window as the brick storefronts of Grayling flashed by outside, large turn-of-the-century monstrosities with elaborately carved cornices spilling over the rooftops like sea foam.

"No," I said, after a moment had passed, because I knew he was still waiting for an answer.

Rain Check

As they walked back to the hotel through the rain-slicked streets of San Francisco, Eddie Ridgeway could tell that his daughter Angela was feeling better. The crying episode in the restaurant was forgotten and she talked excitedly about visiting Alcatraz the next day. She had seen the movie with Burt Lancaster, she said, and it was an amazing place.

Eddie played along. Crossing Union Square he tried some funny gangster imitations—James Cagney and Peter Lorrie—which made her laugh. In front of an open stairwell Angela hunched her shoulders and pretended to spray bullets from a make-believe Tommy gun down into the darkness, making khu-khu-khu sounds deep down in her throat. All of this pleased Eddie very much.

Back in their hotel room Angela got ready for bed while Eddie sat reading a book. After a few minutes she came over and sat on the edge of Eddie's chair. She put an arm around his shoulder.

"So it's Alcatraz tomorrow, right?"

"Right, kiddo."

She leaned her head on his shoulder. "I'm sorry about what happened in the restaurant."

"Don't worry about it."

"I'm such a baby."

"It's perfectly normal."

She hugged him. Eddie felt her warm breath on his neck.

"Do you still think about Mom?" she asked him.

"Of course."

"What do you think about? Now, I mean."

Eddie shifted in his chair. He considered the question. "I suppose it's the memory," he said. "The memory of who she was. The kind of person she was."

They were silent for a moment.

"That's sort of vague," Angela said.

"You know what I mean."

"Tell me what you liked best about her," she asked brightly.

Eddie thought for a moment. He wanted her to understand that it had been a good marriage.

"Well," he said, "for one thing I liked the way she looked, always dressed so nicely. And I liked that she was such a strong person. She knew exactly what she wanted and went right after it. No holding back."

"She *was* like that, wasn't she?"

"Yes."

Eddie waited for the next question but for the moment she seemed satisfied. After a while she rose and got into bed. Eddie said, "Sleep tight and don't let the bed buffaloes bite," a tired line from when she was just a child. She smiled goofily and rolled her eyes and said, "I won't."

Eddie turned out the lights and sat in the chair by the window. Outside, a swirling mist formed droplets on the glass that ran down in jagged sparkling patterns. In the park across from the hotel he saw people strolling on the shiny pathways. A statue on a tall marble pedestal glistened in the streetlights.

It had been four months now, and in spite of what had happened in the restaurant Eddie believed they were doing very well. Bringing Angela along on this business trip had been a good idea. It showed that things were getting back on track, that after four months they were carrying on okay without Anne.

There were many separate parts to grief—Eddie knew that now—but the hardest parts were certainly behind them. They were past the numb, sleepwalk-feeling part and also the panicky, waking-in-the-night part. They were past the part where he and Angela traded small brave smiles whenever their eyes happened to connect and they were past the part where Eddie would suddenly realize, on going up to bed, that they had forgotten to have dinner. They were past the part where Eddie watched despairingly as Angela drifted through the house, a vague smile on her face, lifting and examining small objects—a ceramic ashtray, a brass candlestick, a porcelain figurine—as though she were selecting merchandise in a store. And they were past the part where you fight down sudden tears in the midst of business meetings, backyard barbecues, favorite television shows, and also the part where you brace up against a seizing anger when friends make sympathetic small talk, and also the part where you clinch your fists against sudden and destructive rages. They were past all those parts.

Eddie rose and moved quietly over to Angela's bed. He looked down at his daughter sleeping in the murky half-light. Her long blond hair fanned out across the pillow as if it had been arranged for some artistic effect. One arm angled across her stomach.

Throughout his marriage Eddie had been faithful to his wife. He had been attracted to other women but he had been faithful to Anne. That had been a point of honor with him, something rock hard. But now it was a different story and Eddie understood that. When certain things happen you are allowed to do things differently. Things you thought you would never do were possible to consider.

Eddie stood looking down at his daughter. Then he went over to the desk and found a sheet of hotel stationery. He composed a note saying he would be downstairs in the bar. He creased the paper into a V and set it on the nightstand. Then he quietly opened the door and slipped out into the hallway.

There was some kind of a convention going on, something to do with stocks and investments. Whatever it was, the revelry was making Eddie feel better. The black mood that had started in his room was lifting under the influence of scotch and piano music and the sounds of lively conversations.

Two more of the conventioneers came into the bar, women with peeling nametags clinging to their blouses and loose-leaf binders tucked securely beneath their arms. Eddie watched them standing by the entrance, their gazes working slowly around the crowded room. One was tall, a strawberry blond in a bright green dress; the other wore something black and clingy.

The piano player struck up a new song, a Johnny Mercer piece that Eddie thought he knew; *Moon Dreams*, maybe. Eddie sipped his scotch and listened to the song. He seemed to remember hearing it in another bar, years ago, with Anne. Early in their married life they'd enjoyed those evenings out together, usually staying until the final set was over and the musicians were packing up their instruments. He remembered late-night walks through empty parking lots, the two of them with their arms around each other, a slow lingering kiss before stepping into the car and heading home.

He looked over at the women again. They were sitting at a table now, talking, their heads close together. He watched them for a while, wondering what they were saying. He liked watching them. He liked their serious expressions and he liked the way the redhead held her hair back when she leaned forward to say something to her friend. He liked the sound of their voices, the soft modulations barely audible above the background buzz.

Eddie pulled his gaze away. He thought again about the song and about his marriage. He and Anne had been together for seventeen years and Eddie always said that it had been a good marriage; not perfect, perhaps, in the way that Hollywood makes it look, but really quite good. Like every couple they had occasional disagreements, and once, years ago, there had even been some wild talk about divorce. But they had learned to deal with their problems, to find accommodations, to carry on.

One reason they'd done so well, Eddie thought, was because they'd given each other room to pursue their separate interests. With Anne it was her art groups and political causes, and on Eddie's side it was his engineering career—that, and the basement woodworking shop where he would disappear for hours each evening. True, they had followed different paths, but they had made the marriage work, both of them understanding that when you have a child you do things in certain ways.

Over at the other table the woman in black suddenly stood up. She said something in an angry tone to her companion, then turned and stalked away. The other one—the redhead—looked over at Eddie and grinned and shrugged her shoulders. Then she leaned back and gazed across the room at the piano player.

When the song ended she turned to Eddie and said something.

"What?" Eddie said.

"I said, 'Do you want to buy a mutual fund?'" She raised her voice so it carried over to Eddie's table.

Eddie picked up his drink and went over. "What are you offering?" he asked her. She scrunched her forehead in mock concentration. "Nothing, I guess. They're all losers." Eddie laughed and sat down.

"Are you here for the convention?" the woman asked.

"No," Eddie said. "I'm in town on business."

"Because you look like you could be a stockbroker. That's why I asked."

"I'm an engineer," Eddie said. "I design automation systems for factories."

"That sounds exciting," the woman said. "High tech stuff."

Eddie looked at her, wondering if she was serious. It had been a long time since anyone had been much impressed by his career.

"I'm a broker's assistant," the woman said. "Indianapolis. Merrill Lynch."

"I'm Eddie Ridgeway," he said. "Detroit." He held out

his hand and the woman reached across and grasped it.

"Beverly," she said.

Eddie took a swallow of his drink. Up close, he saw that Beverly was older than he had thought, perhaps forty or forty-five. She had calm, heavy-lidded eyes. A tiny scar cut through one eyebrow.

"Where did your friend go?" he asked.

Beverly made a face. "She's not exactly my friend," she said. "Just some loony-tune agent from Kansas City with husband troubles. I listened to her whining as long as I could stand it." She raised her glass and took a swallow, keeping her calm, dark eyes on Eddie. "I finally told her: 'What do I look like, sweetie, your shrink?' That's exactly what I said. 'I'm here for fun,' I said, 'not psychotherapy.'" She sipped her drink again.

"You're pretty tough," Eddie said.

Beverly half-smiled. "As tough as I need to be," she said. "Anyway, we've all got our own problems, right?"

"Right," Eddie said. He picked up his glass and swirled the ice.

"Who was that pretty girl I saw you with this afternoon?" Beverly asked.

Eddie raised his glance. Beverly had a teasing smile on her face. He decided she was quite drunk.

"You must be thinking of someone else."

"No, it was you all right. With a pretty girl. Downstairs in the lobby."

Eddie cast around in his mind; then he understood. "Oh. You're talking about my daughter, Angela."

Beverly laughed. "You've got a sweetheart there, Eddie. In a couple of years you'll have to fight the boys off with a stick."

Eddie grimaced at the thought of Angela being pursued that way. He didn't like being reminded about how close she was to all of that. It was something he'd have to deal with eventually, but he didn't want to think about it now.

Beverly's gaze drifted over to the piano player. "Where's Angela's mama?" she asked.

"Nowhere," Eddie said. Then, after a moment, he added: "Her mother died four months ago."

Beverly turned and Eddie felt her calm gaze land on him with a certain sympathetic force. "Jeez, I'm sorry," she said. She reached across and touched his arm. He felt the pressure of her fingers through his jacket. "I'm way too nosy," she said.

"It's okay," Eddie said. He pulled back his arm.

They sat quietly, sipping their drinks. At the next table a couple—a woman in an electric blue dress and a heavy man with sideburns—began talking in loud voices. Eddie watched the woman reach across the table and pull the man's glass away. The man grabbed her wrist and said, "Oh, no you don't," and pulled the glass back. Then they both laughed uproariously.

"Two days ago...."

Beverly was saying something. Eddie turned back. She was looking at her watch. "No, wait a minute, I guess it was three." She laughed and shook her head. "Two or three, it doesn't matter. Anyway, I was out on the open waters of the Pacific in a kayak. That's what I'm trying to tell you."

"Kayak," Eddie said.

"One of those little boats where you sit and paddle."

Eddie waited for Beverly to continue but instead she took another swallow of her drink. She was plastered, he decided. Smashed. Three sheets to the wind.

"Where was this?" he asked after a minute had passed.

"What?" She looked at him as if she didn't understand. Then she said: "Oh. It was up the coast in Bodega Bay. I took this kayak three or four miles off-shore to see what it was like."

Eddie didn't know what to make of what she was telling him. None of it made any sense.

"My ex-husband told me about it," Beverly continued. "He did it once and had this experience that changed him in some profound way. Anyway, that's what he told me. So it was something I filed away in my brain to do." She touched an index finger to her temple. "Something I planned to do one day when I wanted a life-changing experience."

Another moment passed in silence. "So what was it like?" Eddie asked.

Beverly gave him a blank stare. Then she shook her head and blinked once or twice. "Oh," she said. "Not too bad, I guess. Kind of peaceful and nice." She stared across the room and narrowed her eyes. "But frightening, too. All alone like that in such a little-bitty boat." She was quiet for a moment, then she laughed.

Eddie looked at Beverly and considered what she'd said. He remembered a summer day when he and Anne had taken a canoe down the Huron River. At one point they had lain back and let the current carry them along, the canoe spinning under the overhanging branches like a leaf caught in a storm drain. Eddie wondered if that was what Beverly was talking about, that sense of giving up to something vast and overpowering.

"Here's a news flash," Beverly said. Eddie looked at her. Her eyes were closed. "Beverly is getting a little tipsy." She rocked her head slowly back and forth. "Beverly needs to get some fresh air." She stood up, one hand gripping the back of the chair.

"Are you all right?" Eddie asked.

"Just peachy," she said. "But if I'm not back in ten minutes send out a scouting party."

She turned and began to make her way across the crowded room, teetering a bit on her high heels. Eddie watched her. Then he rose and followed.

Out on the street Eddie felt the fine cool mist on his face. They walked down to the corner and crossed into the park.

"Feeling better?" he asked her.

"A little," she said. "I don't know what came over me. I'm usually a better soldier."

They followed a pathway to the center of the park and sat on a stone bench beneath the statue. Pockets of gray mist drifted slowly over the ground, like the ghosts of stalking animals.

Beverly shifted a little and leaned her head on Eddie's shoulder. He flinched at the unexpected movement. After a moment he smelled her perfume. Then he felt her hair against his neck.

"Do you like to fish?" she asked.

"Fish? What do you mean?"

"Isn't that what they do in Michigan?"

"Oh, yes," he said. "Some people do. I don't."

"What, then?"

"What?"

"What *do* you do? In your spare time?"

"I have a woodworking shop in my basement. Planes and routers and things. Sometimes I listen to jazz."

"No kidding." She laughed. "Jazz."

Beverly moved a little, as if to make herself more comfortable. Eddie turned his head and had a close-up view of tangled red curls and the wavering line where her hair was parted. He liked the dull pressure of Beverly's head resting on his shoulder.

A young couple strolled by, holding hands and laughing. Then two men came along, dressed in business suits. One of them looked at Eddie, then he looked across the park and said something to his companion. Eddie followed the man's gaze. Through the pockets of drifting fog he saw a fire burning in an oil drum. A group of rough-looking people huddled around it.

"We're all just hanging out together here, aren't we,

Eddie?" Beverly said. She nodded in the direction of the burning barrel. "That's the main thing we've got going for us, I think."

Eddie kept staring at the people gathered around the barrel, thinking about her remark. He wondered if it had something to do with her kayak experience, or if it meant anything at all. Then he wondered what would happen if they went over and joined the group around the barrel. The thought made him smile.

After another minute Beverly stood up. She tipped back her head and shook her long, lopsided curls into position; then she flashed Eddie a big grin.

"Thanks for taking care of me," she said. "Beverly's all better now."

On the way back to the hotel it started to drizzle. Eddie took Beverly's arm and steered her under the canopy of a darkened store. They stood for several minutes looking out at the rain. Then Eddie turned and looked down at her. He remembered the feeling of her hair against his neck and he wondered what would happen if he tried to kiss her. Would she be offended? Or even care? It had been a long time since he'd tried to kiss a woman and he'd forgotten the fine points, the hints and little signals that conveyed interest or intent.

"What was your wife's name?" Beverly asked him.

Eddie looked at her. She was staring out at the street. The headlights of passing cars played over her face, making it look as if she were witnessing some violent spectacle.

"Anne," he said.

"Do you think about her much?"

"Not too much," he answered quickly.

Beverly turned to him with a quizzical expression. "But you loved her, right?"

Eddie looked out at the street. The way she had asked the question, so blunt, made it seem like a completely fresh matter, something he had never actually considered.

Seventeen years. That's how long they had been married. He tried to sum it up, tried to draw a line around it, tried to figure out what it had all meant. He turned back to Beverly. She was still staring at him, searching his face with her calm, steady eyes.

"Our marriage..." He searched to find the words that would express what he remembered, the accommodations, the compromises, the feelings left unvoiced for Angela's sake.

"Our marriage..." he began again. A car sped past, sending up a furious spray of water. Eddie turned and watched it disappear down the street. Then he turned back and faced her.

"We had some problems," he said. "I guess I didn't really love her. Not the way you're supposed to."

Beverly stared at him for a long time. She just stared at him in silence. Then she turned away.

"Would you like to kiss me, Eddie?" She spoke in an

ordinary voice, still looking out. The lights of a passing car flared across her face.

"Kiss you?"

"It's just a thought." She turned to him, a solemn expression on her face. Then she smiled.

"All right," Eddie said. He leaned down and put his arms around Beverly's waist and started to kiss her, gently and with some vague sense of gratitude—and then with greater eagerness, eagerly, her mouth cool, the green dress smooth beneath his hands. And although it had been a long time it was instantly familiar, the accommodating shape, the sweet-smelling skin, the hard-pounding heart, the sudden-building sense of excitement and anticipation.

"Whoa, tiger," Beverly said. She placed a hand on his chest and backed away. The sharp edges of a brick wall dug into the back of Eddie's hand where she pressed back against it.

"Sorry," he said. "I guess I got carried away."

Beverly drew back her face and gave him an amused stare. "I guess you did," she said. "But that's not all bad."

The rain stopped. They walked back to the hotel, holding hands. In the red-carpeted lobby Eddie saw the enormous grandfather clock and the marble columns that went up and up and seemed like they belonged in a church instead of a hotel.

He turned to Beverly. Her damp red curls lay flat against her forehead. He thought she looked very beautiful and he wanted to kiss her again.

"Well," Beverly said, "what's next on the agenda?"

Eddie looked around. Across the lobby, the night manager was giving them a look. From the direction of the bar he heard a sudden peal of laughter. It rolled into the lobby like a giant wave and then receded, leaving behind a peculiar, lonely silence.

"I suppose we could go upstairs to my room and chat for a while," Beverly continued. "Attack the mini-bar. There's some peach schnapps there. Do you like peach schnapps, Eddie?"

"Sure," he said. And then he remembered Angela.

He put his hand on Beverly's arm. He tried to think about what he wanted to say. He knew something was wrong and he knew he needed to change it.

"Look," he said, "what I told you back there on the street about my wife. That was a mistake."

Beverly pulled back a little.

"It wasn't correct," he said. "I don't know what I was thinking."

She looked at him with a puzzled expression. "Maybe it was a momentary lapse of memory?" she said.

"That's right. It was a lapse. A crazy lapse." He looked around as if afraid they might be overheard. Then he added: "I should probably get back upstairs."

Beverly stared at him for a long time without saying anything. Then she stretched out her arms and yawned.

"It's probably for the best," she said. "Beverly should get her beauty rest. We'll take a rain check on further developments."

Eddie stood just inside the doorway to the room, letting his eyes adjust to the cool dim light. Angela lay on her side with one leg drawn up, a fist tucked under her chin. She reminded Eddie of a horizontal version of Rodin's "The Thinker."

The air conditioning fan kicked on, filling the air with a soft electric buzz. Eddie saw his note on the nightstand. He went over and crumpled it up and threw it into the wastebasket. Then he sat down on the edge of Angela's bed.

After a moment she stirred and opened her eyes. She blinked at him two or three times.

"Hello, Daddy."

"Hi, kiddo."

"Is it time to get up?"

"No, sweetheart. It's only the middle of the night. Go back to sleep."

He bent down and kissed her cheek. Her skin was warm and sleep soft. He let his lips rest for a moment in the hollow of her neck, felt the slow, measured pulsing of her heart, the conduit of sweet life pouring through her body.

She grimaced and turned her face away. "You smell like perfume," she murmured sleepily.

He was silent for a moment as he cast about for something to say. "I was downstairs for a while," he said. "I sat and talked with this interesting woman. She was a real character."

"You mean like you went on a date?"

"No. Nothing like that. We just sat and talked in the bar."

"Is that all?"

He waited for a moment before answering. "Well, we went over to the park for a few minutes. She wanted some fresh air."

Angela lifted herself on one elbow. "Did you like her?"

"She was nice. Just a woman."

"But you liked her."

Eddie looked at the floor. He thought about holding Beverly in his arms. Then he pushed the thought away. "Yes, I guess I liked her."

"So maybe you'll fall in love with her."

"I doubt it."

"But you don't know. You can't control those things."

"Yes you can, kiddo. It's not the way you think."

She looked at him with a cloudy expression. Then she lay back down.

"Did you like her better than Mom?"

"It's a different thing, kiddo. I was married to your mom, remember."

Angela's eyes narrowed in a sort of frown. Eddie looked back at her, barely breathing. He heard the muffled sounds of traffic rising up from the street below, then the pneumatic clink of an elevator door closing somewhere. Finally she rolled onto her side.

"Am I a character, too?" she murmured.

"Yes, you are."

"Good." She smiled and closed her eyes.

Eddie sat on the edge of the bed and watched his daughter going back to sleep. His mind was calm now and for the moment he felt released and absolved. What he'd said about Anne had been a mistake; he'd made that clear. He had loved his wife and Angela was the proof of it. To think otherwise would be absurd.

After a while Angela's breathing became steady. Eddie stood and walked over to the window. He looked down into the park. It was almost deserted now but off to one side something caught his eye. When he looked closer he recognized the orange blaze of the burning barrel. He stood and stared, watched the flames rise and fall, stroking the sky in bright erratic bursts. He could just make out the red-tinged faces of the people gathered around it. They reminded him of the survivors of a shipwreck, lost souls huddling on some dangerous, inhospitable shore.

Behind him Eddie heard a noise. He turned around. Angela was rolling back and forth on the bed, struggling against the tangled sheets, caught in the grip of some vivid and overpowering dream. Eddie thought that he should wake her. But then she suddenly stopped struggling and sat up and stared blindly across the room, her eyes puffy, sleep-glazed, uncomprehending. And then as Eddie watched she raised a hand and touched it gently to her face, felt the contour of her cheek, her nose, her mouth, her chin, as though she were examining something delicate and profound, something inexpressibly rare, something that was meant for Eddie's eyes alone.

Speaking of Love Abstractly

Because of the unfamiliar language (fitful bursts of tortured French); because of the coffee house filled with university students; because of the slightly dissolute atmosphere (they always choose the smoking section where she could enjoy her Marlboros); because of the afternoon hours stolen from his law office; because of the pretty young *Française* sitting across the table from him laughing (occasionally) at his stories and looking so unlike the woman to whom he had been married for twenty-seven years—because of all these things and others Harold Elliot began to feel as though he had stepped into a different life, or become a different person, or perhaps both things together. He began to have feelings for her—he could not help it—and so he put sly messages into the *récits* he prepared for each week's lesson. At first they were vague comments about the superiority of French culture (where he could reasonably make a case for that), and then they were directed more particularly toward Mademoiselle Carnot herself: her appearance (dark unruly hair fetched up with a tortoise-shell clip, steady-gazing brown eyes, small mouth outlined in an unlikely shade of pink); the styles that she favored (a leopard skin beret; bulbous, wraparound sunglasses that looked like insect eyes; leather gloves with ventilator holes in back); the soft staccato of her voice; her sharp whoop of laughter that sounded like a siren going off (she had smiled at this and blushed).

"You are doing much better," she said one day. (*On parle beaucoup mieux.*) They were working their way through the opening chapters of *Bonjour Tristesse,* the Françoise Sagan novel about the concurrent love affairs of a seventeen-year old girl and her middle-aged father, scandalous when it was published in 1953 but now seeming quite tame. "I'm very impressed by your prog-ress." (*Votre progrès m'impressionne.*) She tilted back her chair and regarded him. Her insect-eye sunglasses were perched atop her head, looking like the raised visor of a helmet. "You must be studying very hard." (*Vous devez étudier dur.*)

"I have quite a bit of free time these days," he said, relapsing into English.

"Oh," she said, "doesn't your wife make demands on your time?" She tipped forward and began to gather up her papers.

"Actually, we've been separated for a few months." He massaged the back of his neck. "*Nous nous sommes séparés.*"

"Oh, how fucking sad," she said, and Harold smiled, her innocent, indiscriminate use of profanity being one of the things about her he found charming.

Mademoiselle Carnot stood up, hefted the strap of her book bag onto her shoulder, reached up and dropped her sunglasses into place.

"Those things happen," he said.

"I suppose," she said, and she smiled her bright pink smile. "Same time next week?"

"Right," he said.

"*À la prochaine,*" she said, turning away.

"Right," he said, watching her. "*À la prochaine.*"

Each Sunday morning Harold returned to the house on Walnut Street where he had breakfast with Marjorie. It was a ritual they began in May, a final beachhead on the terrain of their almost-ruined marriage. As with the separation itself, it had been Marjorie's idea, suggested in a telephone call a few days after she had tearfully requested that Harold remove himself from the house. It was one of several logistical matters they settled that night, the others being the setting up of separate bank accounts, his access to the fishing gear in the basement (that could not be accommodated in his new studio apartment), and his thoughts about how she might locate a repairman for the garage door opener.

This morning they sat on the patio in the warm, late-fall sunshine, reading the *Tribune,* occasionally catching the other's eye and smiling in a vague, broken-hearted way. The remnants of breakfast lay scattered on the table: crumpled napkins, empty eggshells, brittle shards of toast. Marjorie put down her section of the paper and looked across at Harold. She had known for several weeks about his French language lessons.

"So what's it all about?" she asked him. "This French girl."

"It's something I've always wanted to do," Harold said. "Become fluent in French. I studied it in high school." He turned a page. "No big deal."

He had spotted Mademoiselle Carnot's sign on the community bulletin board at the Kroger's where he shopped each Friday for bread and cold cuts. "Learn French the French way," the sign proclaimed in large red letters, and in smaller ones below: "(from a French person)."

He had stood for a moment, fingering the little sign, and his mind had filled with a jumble of images: Paul Cézanne trudging Provençal hills, Jean-Paul Sartre arguing at *Le Dôme*, World War II resistance fighters blowing up a bridge, vineyards in Bordeaux.

"I think I understand," Marjorie said, a teasing note in her voice. "A little French girlfriend to spice things up."

Harold put down the newspaper and looked out at the

back yard. Sunlight through the leaves spotted the ground in moving patterns. He hated when Marjorie went into her mocking personality. It was one of several she affected these days, putting them on and taking them off like she tried out clothes before a party.

"Come on, Marge," he said, "she's a graduate student, for crying out load. In architecture."

"That's what I mean," she said. "It makes no sense."

Harold folded his newspaper, folded it again, then set it on the table. He took a sip of his coffee, looking over the rim at the birdbath shimmering in the sunshine like a tiny mirage.

She had grown up in Lyon, her father a well-to-do industrialist and her mother the head of a foundation that sent aid missions to Africa. After the university in Paris she had married a ski instructor from St. Moritz and had trained for a time with the French luge team, aiming for the next Olympics. But the marriage had ended in some unhappy way and a crash on the fifth turn at Innsbruck had ruined her Olympic chances as well as her left knee.

"So I gave up the sporting life and went back to school. One has to do something, right?" She sat in the coffee house with her injured leg resting on an empty chair, a casualty of the damp Chicago weather. "Now I will make buildings. Big American buildings in France."

"What happened to your husband?"

She made a face. "I left him because he was a shit. Or maybe I was." She shrugged. "Who knows?"

"Why Chicago?"

She ticked off the reasons on her fingers: "Skyscrapers, Frank Lloyd Wright, the Art Museum with the stolen French impressionists, and the big-shouldered workers." She smiled. "Also, I can tutor French and earn money."

"I thought your father was rich."

"In France being rich means something different."

"Oh," he said, nodding.

A moment passed. Harold stirred his coffee. His mind filled with an image of Mademoiselle Carnot hurtling down a twisting white-glazed groove of ice, her body encased in a shiny plastic film—then an awful screech, screams, a blood-soaked mound of snow.

"What's this?" She leaned forward and pulled an official-looking paper from between the pages of his Sagan novel.

"It's a parking ticket I got years ago when my wife and I were vacationing in Paris. I use it as a bookmark."

She studied it, a squint creasing the corners of her eyes and mouth. "*Quelle coïncidence*," she said. "I was born the day you got this." She smiled brightly. "It's my birthday."

He reached and took the ticket from her hand, noted the date: May 12, 1972. "Well, isn't that amazing," he said.

"Yes, it is," she said, and laughed. "It's fucking amazing."

He fingered the paper, remembering the night he and Marjorie had trudged the darkened streets of the sixth district looking for the parking lot where the gendarmes took impounded cars. Three hundred miles away this young woman was being born. It *was* amazing.

"Look at this," she said suddenly. She pulled up her pant leg. "This fucking knee."

Harold leaned forward and examined it. An ugly red scar circled Mademoiselle Carnot's kneecap. Along both edges were small irregular slashes, a sort of waffle pattern.

"In the United States," he said, "the doctors use special stitches that dissolve." He gestured toward her knee. "They don't leave marks."

"How wonderful," she said. "Americans are so lucky."

Harold saw her eyes brimming with tears and he politely dropped his gaze. Not knowing where else to look he regarded her knee again. He remembered nights spent keeping watch over childhood cases of measles, chicken pox, a broken arm.

"Does this help?" He began to massage the place where the kneecap seemed most ruined.

"Yes," she said, smiling bravely through a mist of tears. "A little."

The separation had come in March, a year after Harold's angioplasty and six months to the day after Angela, the second and last of their children, had left for college in California. It followed an ugly period marked by Marjorie's wild swings of temperament and Harold's menacing silences. Without the distractions of their children it seemed they could no longer stand to be around each other. All the old accommodations—the little disciplines that had made their lives tolerable, even enjoyable, for so many years—were suddenly gone.

They had married too young, that much was now clear, when, for a brief, ill-considered time they had thought that Marjorie's Toronto roots might give Harold an immunity from the Vietnam draft, a sort of leg-up on Canadian citizenship that would not require that he actually go to live in that cold country. Quickly enough they learned that the ploy would not work, but they were left to deal with the consequences of their rash act, which included the fact that they did not really know each other very well. Still, they had gamely pushed forward with their joined lives and things had worked out well enough, or at least not bad—careers, children, a series of ever-larger houses— no better or worse, Harold supposed, than most other marriages. But after twenty-seven years the old problem had come back. In the stillness of their child-bereft house Harold would sometimes look at Marjorie and wonder who she was, and how they had come to occupy the same space together.

Alone one night in his new studio apartment, Harold thought back over the years. He was a careful man who believed life was filled with risk. At his law firm he specialized in government contracts, disputes among bureaucrats about tanks and battleships and paper clips. He was known as a lawyer's lawyer, a man to whom others brought their most vexing cases, who could look dispassionately and find the thread that would unravel a legal mess. He had known success (his name was attached to several obscure points of law) but he had made many compromises, had probably not fought or loved enough, or well enough, which was perhaps the same thing.

Harold went into the tiny kitchenette and poured himself a glass of bourbon. He returned and stood for a moment looking around the darkened room—a 12-inch television rested on a cardboard box in one corner, a goose-necked lamp dropped a circle of light onto stacks of legal briefs, a threadbare sofa sat against one wall—and then his gaze traveled out the window to a parking lot studded with streetlamps. As Harold watched, a tiny sports car came slowly down an aisle and fit itself into an empty space beneath his window. The occupants, a young man and woman, got out and disappeared into the building, their arms around each other.

Harold sipped his drink.

Where had it come from, he wondered, this desire to be alone, to stand in the dark and watch couples walk through parking lots, to do without, to punish himself, as if he had committed some awful crime that he alone had knowledge of?

Harold sipped his drink again. A moment passed. He saw no other signs of life.

Ever since his angioplasty operation Harold never went anywhere without half expecting that he would not come back alive. He carried a cell phone with emergency numbers programmed for instant activation. In his breast pocket rested a tiny vial of nitroglycerin tablets. His wallet ID was up-to-date with next of kin and various doctors, specialists in heart, lungs, broken legs. Dog tags hung from a chain around his neck, announcing his blood type and medications.

On Thursday he saw his doctor. "There's this little thing in my shoulder," he said. "Sort of a twitch."

The doctor moved the stethoscope to another spot on Harold's chest, narrowed his eyes. Harold breathed in, tried to relax, focused on the gaudy diplomas hanging on the examination room wall, fancy Latin words rendered in gilded script.

"What kind of twitch?" the doctor asked.

"A sort of jumping thing. Like a muscle spasm. Only very small."

The doctor moved the stethoscope again.

"It comes and goes," Harold said. "Like a hummingbird is in there."

The doctor removed the stethoscope. "A what?" he said.

"A hummingbird," Harold said. "It feels like a humming-bird."

"Oh," the doctor said. He set the stethoscope on a metal table, the rubber tubes coiling like a nest of snakes. He began to write something in Harold's folder. "I wouldn't worry," he said.

Harold watched him write. Ever since his angioplasty Harold had the feeling his doctor was keeping something from him, most likely knowledge of some hopeless condition that could not be treated and thus would serve no purpose to disclose. "I just thought I should mention it," he said weakly.

"Of course," the doctor said, still writing. "It doesn't hurt to mention things."

Harold stood up and began to button his shirt.

"What about sex?" he said.

"What?" The doctor stopped writing and looked up.

"Sex," Harold said. "Is that all right? For me, I mean. In my condition."

"Sure," said the doctor. "Why not?"

"No reason," Harold said. "I just thought I'd ask."

The next week he followed Mademoiselle Carnot to her apartment to borrow a text on French slang. At each stoplight his Ford Explorer loomed up behind her Honda Civic and she would look up and waggle her fingers at him in the rear view mirror, a bit of silliness that touched him deeply. In the small space she rented on the second-floor of a parceled-up Victorian mansion she set out wine and cheese and apple wedges and they discussed the latest news accounts from France: the progress toward the thirty-five hour work week, the schism in *Le Front National*, Gérard Dépardieu's latest film, the farmers' strike.

Harold sat on a pile of giant pillows that seemed to be the main furnishings in the room. Mademoiselle Carnot sat cross-legged on the floor, her wine glass balanced on her good knee, a cigarette pinned between two stiff fingers. She had unclipped her hair and it lay about her shoulders in a profusion of loose tangles, as if a black, airy cloud had come to settle on her shoulders. Harold wondered if the gesture could be interpreted as an encouragement, but he had chosen not to pursue that thought very far.

"I don't get it," he said to her now. "Someone is always striking in France. Even the farmers go on strike."

"Yes," she said, "so what? They are communists. That's what they do."

"The farmers are communists?"

"In France they are. Some." Harold shook his head. "And this business about a thirty-five hour work week. What's that all about?"

"It's simple," she said. She exhaled a jet of cigarette smoke from the corner of her mouth. "It helps the economy. It makes full employment."

Harold looked away. In the darkened space beyond a partly opened doorway he saw the eerie glow of a tropical fish tank. It seemed to float in mid-air, a bright rectangle throwing a greenish cast onto an unmade bed littered with clothes.

He turned back to Mademoiselle Carnot, breathed in a quantity of air. "I have a function to go to next Wednesday night," he said. "It's sort of a charity dinner. Walter Cronkite is speaking." Harold rubbed the corner of his eye distractedly. "Maybe you could come along."

Mademoiselle Carnot looked down into her glass. She swirled it so that the wine lapped up against the sides. "Who's Walter Cronkite?" she said.

"He's a famous TV newscaster. But he's retired now."

She swirled her wine again. "A free meal. Why not?"

"It's sort of dressy," he said. "Not that that's important."

She expelled another jet of smoke, grinned. "You mean I should wear nice clothes. Don't worry. I have some."

"I'm sure you do," he said, feeling slightly flustered.

"I won't embarrass you," she said. "I'll be fucking ravishing."

They made their slow way down the rickety staircase of her apartment building.

"Never do the luge," she said. "That's just my opinion."

At the curbside he held up the text on French slang. "Thanks for loaning this to me," he said.

"Sure," she said. Then, "Here, this is how friends say good-bye in France." She stepped forward, reached up, bussed him quickly on the left cheek, then the right, barely a touch. "It's a cultural thing," she said. "You should learn it."

Harold looked down at her, considered for an instant taking her into his arms ("*This is how we do it in America.*") but did not. Instead he got into his car and pulled away, watching her image diminish slowly in the rear view mirror.

❋   ❋   ❋

They were on their way to the renovated 1920s movie theater where the charity affair was being held, passing through a particularly disreputable section of the city. Mademoiselle Carnot reached across from the passenger's side and fingered a tiny aluminum bracelet on Harold's wrist. "What's this?" she asked.

"It's nothing," Harold said. He removed his hand from the steering wheel and rotated his wrist so his shirt cuff worked lower on his arm and covered the bracelet.

"It's *something*," she said. "I know something when I see it."

"It's just a bracelet. It says they can harvest my organs."

"Harvest?" Mademoiselle Carnot mouthed the word several times. Then she whispered *"récolter,"* as though the French version might disclose some meaning that escaped her in the English. "Like a fruit orchard?" she said, hesitantly. "Apples and cherries and plums."

"Sort of," he said. "It says that if something happens— let's say there's a serious accident and I'm killed—then they can take my bodily organs and use them for someone else." He looked at her. "Harvest them."

She turned and stared out the side window. Boarded-up storefronts slid by, their dark surfaces periodically relieved by bright splashes of graffiti.

"This is serious?" she said.

"Of course it's serious," he said. "You never know when something terrible might happen."

They stopped for a red light. "Let me out!" Mademoiselle Carnot said suddenly. She edged away from him, clutching dramatically at the door handle.

"What are you talking about?"

"I don't want to be here when it happens. The terrible thing."

The light went green. Harold began to pull forward. "You can't get out here. It's too dangerous."

They rolled on through the intersection. "I was only kidding," she said. "*Seulement une blague.*" Beneath the glare of a streetlight a group of people stood with hunched shoulders. "Besides," she added, "maybe I can get your knee."

He had memorized a poem by Rilke and he wanted to recite it for her at some private moment during the evening. It was not a love poem, although it spoke of love abstractly. Reciting it would show a certain side of him, perhaps move their relationship in a different direction, beyond friendship, to a new level of intimacy and trust. But as they drove along Harold began to have doubts. He feared he did not know her well enough, did not know if she liked poetry. He wondered if the gesture might seem staged, premeditated, too much like a ploy.

When they arrived at the old theater a crowd already filled the enormous ornate lobby. Waitresses in black dresses drifted between knots of people in tuxedos and evening dresses, dispensing *canapés* and drinks from silver trays.

Harold found the coat-check room and handed over Mademoiselle Carnot's wrap, then turned back to examine what she was wearing. A bright green dress, frilly at its edges, showed off generous quantities of her legs and shoulders and breasts. "Do you like it?" she asked him, smiling sweetly. "Not bad, *non*?"

"It's fine," he said. "*Sympathique.*"

They edged their way into the crowded lobby. Harold looked around for a secluded corner where he might recite his poem, but then he saw that Mademoiselle Carnot was pressing forward without him, and so he followed. When they reached the center of the lobby she stopped and craned her neck to examine the elaborate ceiling. Fifty feet above their heads plaster storm clouds threatened and gargoyles glowered in hues of bright blue, gold, and red.

"This is no grand thing of architecture," she said, with a sniff.

"It's an American classic," he said. "A 1920s movie house returned to its former glory."

"It's a little gaudy," she said. She reached out and snagged a wedge of Camembert from a passing waiter.

They stood in the middle of the throng of people. Someone jostled Harold and he moved a half step in Mademoiselle Carnot's direction, noticing for the first time a tiny scar that notched her left eyebrow. The sound of a thousand conversations made a steady background roar, like waves breaking against a rocky shore. Harold looked around. It was not a private moment but he thought perhaps it was as good as he would have that night. He leaned in Mademoiselle Carnot's direction. "Do you like poetry?" he asked her.

"Poetry? Yes." She bit a corner of the cheese wedge, regarded him with her wide brown eyes.

"Do you know Rilke?"

"Of course. A German who wrote in French."

"Listen to this," he said, and he leaned down so that his mouth was near to her ear.

"*Ne parlons pas de toi*," he began, a little too suddenly.

"What?" she said, moving closer. "Say it again." The buzz of conversations rose around them. He felt the brush of her hair on his cheek.

"*Ne parlons pas de toi*," he repeated, in a slightly louder voice.

"Yes," she said, "I get it." She held her hair back from her ear.

"*Tu es ineffable selon ta nature.*"

"Yes," she said, nodding. "An indefinable person. I understand."

Harold paused to recall the next line.

"*D'autres fleurs ornent la table que tu transfigures.*"

"Other flowers are on the table," she said. "Yes."

Harold licked his lips. He began to wonder if the poem was such a good idea after all. Somehow it did not feel quite right and for a moment he considered abandoning his plan. And then he felt a slight fluttering begin in his shoulder.

"*On te met dans un simple vase,*" he blurted.

"That's nice," she said. "Pretty flowers go into a plain vase."

The fluttering became stronger, like the thrusts of a hummingbird's wings. Harold swallowed hard and to steady himself he placed a hand on Mademoiselle Carnot's bare shoulder. The warmth of her skin calmed him for a moment and allowed him to carry on.

"*Voici que tout change.*"

"Now everything changes," she said. "How interesting."

Harold scanned the room for a possible escape route, if one became necessary, and he noticed an acquaintance, Emory Arnold, regarding them with a strange, disbelieving expression. Turning his attention back to Mademoiselle Carnot he saw a frown creasing her perfect forehead. He wondered if she could tell that something was wrong with him. But then he thought that perhaps she was only anticipating the next line of his poem, and so he said it.

"*C'est peut-être la même phrase.*"

"But it's still the same," she murmured. "That's puzzling."

Harold struggled to remember what came next, but he was beginning to lose his hold on things. He tried to focus, but the sensation in his shoulder was becoming stronger. Beads of sweat dotted his forehead and his breath came in little gasps.

He braced himself, pressed down harder on Mademoiselle Carnot's shoulder, and finished.

"*Mais chantée par un ange.*"

Mademoiselle Carnot arched her eyebrows and emitted a tiny gasp of pleasure or surprise. "Oh!" she said, "an angel. A singing angel!"

Harold took a deep breath, held it for a moment, then exhaled slowly. "There's another stanza," he said, hoarsely. "But I can't remember it right now."

"That's okay," Mademoiselle Carnot said happily, "it was perfect just the way you said it," and there seemed to be a new quality in her voice, a warmth and a resonance that had not been there before—and Harold understood that he had caused it.

Just then a sudden movement on the other side of the room caught Harold's attention. Looking closer, he saw Walter Cronkite standing in the center of a group of people, nodding and smiling in a wan, long-suffering way. And then the room began to move, a slow glacial drift to the right.

"Is that Walter Cronkite?" Mademoiselle Carnot asked, craning her neck to get a better look. Harold turned back to her. She was smiling, her face alert with Gallic curiosity.

Harold nodded, staggered a bit, and took a faltering step backward. He removed his hand from her shoulder and raised it to his forehead, like a man who has been blessed with a sudden good idea, and slumped slowly to the floor.

They seemed to be in some kind of maintenance room. Bare pipes criss-crossed overhead and a large electrical panel hung on one wall. Harold lay on an Army cot, a stack of newspapers supporting his head. Mademoiselle Carnot sat a little ways away on a cardboard box, legs crossed, peering through a partly-opened doorway into the giant theater lobby.

Harold propped himself on an elbow. "What happened?" he asked.

She came over and knelt down beside him. "You conked out," she said. "Like a light."

With an effort Harold got himself into a sitting position. "They brought you in here," she continued, "after they figured out it wasn't serious. There was a doctor. He said your heart was going too fast. Walter Cronkite came over, too."

"Walter Cronkite?" She helped him to his feet.

"He was very concerned about you. Such a nice man."

Harold rubbed his forehead. He remembered reciting the poem but he could not recall what had happened next. "I feel foolish," he said.

"Don't be," she said. "I told everybody you had been drinking."

Harold took a hesitant step in the direction of the doorway. But then he stopped and turned back to face Mademoiselle Carnot. He felt tired and old and worn out, and he wanted to tell her something that would dispel the foolishness of the poem, explain the idiocy of having recited it, but he could think of nothing. "Maybe we should call it a night," he said instead.

The guests had begun to move into the dining room, leaving the lobby a vast expanse of empty red carpet. Crossing it, Harold looked around again at the extravagant art deco decor. In spite of his condition, he was struck by the audacity of the place, the boldness of spirit it spoke to.

"In America we like to do things big," he murmured, as if he were talking to himself.

"Big," Mademoiselle Carnot said, coming along behind. "In France we have Versailles. That's big."

"It's different," Harold said, with a distracted wave. "Different times, different cultures."

"Things change," she said. "I agree with that."

"Westerns were big back then," Harold said, thinking now about the heyday of the theater, and of his own lost youth. "Gene Autry, Roy Rogers, Hopalong Cassidy."

She looked at him oddly.

"And adventure movies," he continued. "Those were big, too. Tarzan, Flash Gordon, Superman."

"In France we have Obélix," she offered tentatively. "And Astérix."

"It's not the same," he said with some heat. "That's satire."

They reached the coat check area and Harold turned to face her. Her eyes were wide with expectation. And he suddenly remembered the little gasp his poem had provoked in her, and for an instant he wondered if he should try reciting it again. But then he felt another moment of unsteadiness—a residue of his fast-beating heart—and for the second time that night he reached out and placed his hand on Mademoiselle Carnot's bare shoulder—"*Attention!*" she called out, and with a graceful dip she positioned herself beneath his outstretched arm—and he felt again the warmth of her. It was a softness like a baby's and it caused him to think of the *Lyonnaise* child who was starting life the night he lost his car in Paris, and to consider the magic of that, their disparate lives improbably linked together then and now, and he wanted more than ever then to hold her—simply hold her—just as he was doing now, and to contemplate that startling fact together.

Treasure Hunt

Friday night, a long time ago, 1964. I was upstairs in my bedroom doing homework. Later, I planned to get together with my girlfriend, Julie. It wasn't exactly a date but we had talked about getting together to have some fun.

Downstairs, my father and Gary were talking in the kitchen. Gary was home from jail on a weekend furlough. It was a little reprieve my father had arranged with the Washtenaw County sheriff, probably helped along by a small contribution to the local Sportsmans' Club. Or perhaps it wasn't such a small contribution and perhaps it didn't go to the Sportsmans' Club; maybe it went to the sheriff himself. But that didn't matter because Gary wasn't a hardened criminal. He was just a college kid who had taken some things from a sporting goods store—skin diving equipment, for Christ's sake: air tanks and regulators, wet suits and fins—all the paraphernalia for going under water. On Wednesday he would be in court and they would decide what to do with him.

"You're just going to have to get through this, Gary." My father's voice carried up the curving staircase, heavy with authority and good sense. In a little while, he and my mother would be leaving to attend some glittery affair at the country club, but for now he was dispensing his wisdom to Gary. "You might as well make up your mind about having to get through it," he repeated.

"That's exactly what I'm trying to do." Gary's voice was high pitched and strained. "But I don't know how long they're going to give me. That's the hard part."

"I assume it won't be too long. One month. Maybe two. I can't imagine anything longer than two."

"Since when are you an expert about these things?"

"I'm not an expert. I don't pretend to be an expert. But I know what's reasonable."

My father was a stockbroker at Merrill Lynch in Detroit. He had done this all his working life. At parties, friends joked about how much money he made for them. So I guess that meant he was pretty good. Careful and analytical.

I heard a chair scrape across the floor, then footsteps.

"Would you like a coffee or a soft drink?" It was my father's voice again.

"No."

"Well, I'm going to make some coffee." I heard water running. "I'll make enough so that you can have some later."

"Do whatever you want."

I closed my book and pushed back from the desk. I began to think about Julie and the night ahead. I was seventeen and had not slept with a girl but I believed it might happen with Julie. At school dances, she held tight against me, pressed her mouth into the crook of my neck and made little murmuring sounds that I understood to be a sort of promise. Last week, parked in the driveway of her house, she let me move my hand inside her blouse and let it stay there for a long, suspended moment before finally pulling away.

"You know, Gary, when this is all over you can pick up with your life again. You can go back to your music studies and everything will be fine. This is just an interruption of your musical career. Consider it in that light."

"I don't want everything to be the same," Gary said. I think he was crying now. Anyway, he was speaking in a very low voice.

"But it's true," my father said. "I want you to think about that."

After a while I heard the front door open and close, followed by the muffled roar of my father's big El Dorado coming to life in the driveway. I was anxious to see Julie, but first I had to figure out what to do about Gary. Earlier in the day, my parents had taken me aside and told me they didn't want him left alone. I thought it was an odd request—Gary was my older brother, after all—but I assumed they had good reason. There was probably a rule that a person on furlough from prison had to be supervised. It made sense to me that there would be a rule like that.

Suddenly I began to hear violin music, big, powerful sounds that seemed to rush up the stairwell and fill my room like a curdling fog. I left my bedroom and went downstairs. Gary was standing in his familiar spot beside the grand piano, his thin body angled forward, his eyes half closed, one hand working the bow and the other racing back and forth along the frets like a frantic animal seeking shelter.

My brother was a concert-grade violinist. Maybe that's not the right word—concert-grade—but that's how it always seemed to me. As if he could slip into a tuxedo and step onto the stage at Carnegie Hall any time he wanted to. At eleven he could play without interruption a song he had heard on the radio, closing his eyes and picking his way among the notes as if guided by some magical force. By fourteen he was composing works of his own; not masterpieces, perhaps, but accomplished works in their own peculiar way.

I watched Gary from the doorway. Finally he came to a quieter passage. The little animals stopped their frightened scurrying.

"Bravo!" I shouted, and I started to clap.

Gary's eyes snapped open. He stopped his song abruptly,

as though I had caught him in some shameful act.

"Keep going," I said, "it sounds great."

But instead of starting to play again he reached for a cigarette burning in the notch of a crystal ashtray sitting on the piano. "You only think it's good because you don't understand it," he said. "To someone who knows music, it's shit."

"Well, it sounded good to me." I stepped into the room and sat down in my father's big upholstered chair.

"You all right?" I asked.

"Never better." Gary took a drag on his cigarette, cupping his hand as if he were standing in a strong wind.

"I heard Dad giving you a hard time."

"You know how he is. He wants everything to be perfect."

"I guess you can't blame him for that."

"Oh, yeah?" Gary said. "Just watch me."

I half-stood and reached for Gary's cigarettes lying on the piano. I shook one out and lit it, thinking about the new Gary who was sitting in front of me, the one who would be going back to jail on Sunday afternoon. My father liked to say that Gary's music connected our family to the finer things of life. That it showed we occupied a certain place in the world, and proved that Gary and I were destined for better things than to be carpenters or shoe salesmen, which were the jobs my uncles held. But now all that had changed. The finer things of life were not high on Gary's current agenda. He had gotten himself into a hard situation and he seemed to be hardening with it.

"Why'd you do it?" I asked, extinguishing the match with a snap of my wrist. "Take that skin diving stuff."

Gary smiled. "That's a hard one, Wayne. Why do people do anything?"

"Don't bullshit me," I said.

Gary looked down at the backs of his hands, spreading the fingers as if he were examining them for damage. "If you really want to know, brother, it was part of a plan. I was going to search for sunken treasure off the coast of Mexico. I have a book that shows where all the old ships went down."

"That's crazy," I said. "Nobody ever finds that stuff."

"Maybe not. But at least it'd get me out of here."

I stared at Gary, trying to figure out what was going on inside his head. As far as I could see his life was pretty good. In the suburban community where we lived he was a local celebrity, the adored boy genius. His violin playing was featured at school assemblies and civic events, like the time when Richard Nixon came to town to give a speech about the Russians. One summer he had played at all the services at the Presbyterian Church, blasting out "Rock of Ages" and "The Old Rugged Cross" with a fervor that brought tears to the eyes of old ladies in the congregation.

But I didn't want to think about those things now. I had my own problems to worry about. Like how I was going to see Julie and keep an eye on Gary at the same time.

"I'm going to get together with my girlfriend tonight," I said. I examined the tip of my cigarette, as if the burning ash might tell me something. "Maybe she can get a friend for you."

Gary looked at me from behind the giant piano. I watched his upside-down reflection in the shiny black enamel.

"You mean a blind date?" he said.

"Something like that."

He raised the violin and played a few odd notes. "Will it be worth my while?"

"What do you mean by that?"

"Is she blonde? Does she have big breasts?"

I laughed. "There's no guarantees," I said. "I'm sure she'll have *some* breasts. Right now, she's an unknown factor."

Gary smiled for the first time and that made me feel good. Just because he was headed for prison didn't mean he shouldn't have some fun.

"A little romance before Gary goes to jail," he said, still smiling. "Sounds good to me, brother."

I stood and snubbed out my cigarette in the crystal ashtray. "Well, okay," I said. "Let's go."

Julie's house had one of those big covered porches like they have on older houses. A light rain was falling, and as we walked up from the car I saw her standing back in the shadows. When we got closer she stepped out from her hiding place and stood at the top of the steps. She was wearing a bright yellow raincoat with a hood. The porch light reflected off the raincoat in a thousand little slivers of white.

"This is my brother, Gary," I said, looking up at Julie. "He's home from college on a visit."

"*Bonsoir,* Gary," Julie said. Her voice from deep inside her rain hood sounded hollow and strange. "Are you as crazy as Wayne?"

"Crazier," he said.

"Then I like you already," she said.

I went up the steps and gave Julie a kiss. Then, with my hands still around her waist, I explained the idea about getting a girl for Gary. When I finished she arched her eyebrows and drew back her face. "It's kind of late," she said.

"I know." I looked back at Gary. He was standing with his arms crossed, staring up at us. I turned back to Julie and made a face. "Can't you call a friend?" I asked.

Julie pursed her lips in a caricature of deep thought. "I'd like to," she said. "But it's kind of an insult, *n'est pas*? To call a girl at the last minute."

I let go of Julie and went back down to where Gary was standing on the sidewalk. I explained to him about the friend, about how it was too late to do anything. I thought he'd be mad but all he did was turn to Julie and give her a sheepish grin, as though to say that it had been my idea from the start. Something out of his control.

"So what do we do now?" I asked. It seemed to me the rain was coming down harder. I felt it running out of my hair and into my eyes.

"Why don't we go for a walk in the rain?" Julie said. "All three of us."

For a minute nobody said anything. I turned toward Gary and gave him a hard stare, trying to send him a message. I wanted him to leave now, to take the car and go someplace so I could be alone with Julie. I'd done the best I could to get him a girl and it hadn't worked out. What more could he expect?

"Well?" Julie said.

I kept my hard stare on Gary.

"Sounds okay to me," Gary said, looking up at Julie.

We walked for a while without saying anything—Julie and me in front, Gary coming along behind—and then Julie started to ask Gary about his life at college. When he got around to telling her he was a music major she suddenly got very excited.

"That's wonderful!" she said. She turned around to face him. "I love music."

"Really?" Gary said. He spoke as though the fact that amazed him.

"Yes, *really*," she said, laughing. "In fact, I truly believe that music is the only hope for mankind. If it weren't for music we'd all go ka-boom in a second."

"You mean the bomb?" I said to her.

"Exactimondo, *mon ami*." She turned around again. "Don't you think I'm right about that, Gary?"

"I don't know," Gary said from behind. "Maybe."

I looked over at Julie, but all I could see was the yellow hood with sparkling drops of water running down. "Well, if you've got a better idea then let's hear it," she said.

Gary was quiet for a moment. Then he said: "I don't know what the most important thing is."

"*Quel ennui*," Julie said. "You must have some opinion."

Gary was silent again. But finally he spoke. "Love," he said. "I guess I'd say that love's the most important thing."

I looked at Julie. She turned to me and smiled so that the corners of her eyes crinkled. Her face was wet and shiny from the rain. "Now we're getting some place," she said.

We walked along. Above our heads wet tree branches glistened blackly in the streetlamps. I felt the rain seeping into my clothes, damp and cold and heavy. Then Julie started to hum a tune.

"That's Tchaikovsky," Gary said.

"Exactimondo," Julie said. She started to hum again.

"Gary plays the violin," I said. "He's great. Just like Jascha Heifitz."

"No kidding," Julie said. She turned around and started walking backward so she could look at Gary. "Can I hear you some time? Maybe when you're home from college next?"

"I don't play much for other people," Gary said.

"When do you?" Julie said.

"What?" said Gary.

"*When* do you come home from college next? So I can hear you play."

"It'll be a while," he said. "I'm not exactly sure." And I knew from his voice that he was thinking about Wednesday, and what was going to happen to him then.

"You *will* let me know though," she said. "Promise?"

Gary was quiet for a long time. Then he said, "Yes, I promise."

"Great," Julie said, and I could tell she meant it.

Up ahead a man came toward us with a German shepherd. When he saw us he crossed the street so he could pass along on the other side. The big dog barked and lurched against its leash.

"We don't have the plague, mister," Gary called out.

"I'm just trying to keep my dog under control," the man yelled back.

"Take it easy," I said to Gary.

We had been circling the block and were coming back up to Julie's house. The globe on her porch light shined dimly through the rain like a ship's beacon. I decided I'd had enough of walking in the rain and all the talk about music. I wanted to go to a bowling alley or to Jimmy's Drive-In on Woodward Avenue. Someplace where we could have some fun. But my clothes were soaked and I was beginning to feel cold and a little depressed. Nothing about the night seemed right. Without a girl for Gary the evening was pretty much ruined.

"I suppose we should go," I said.

"Can't you come in for a while?" Julie said.

"No," I said, and I guess the word came out sharper than I intended, because Julie turned and looked at me with a hurt expression. "All right," she said, "if *that's* the way you feel." And then she came up close and I felt her cool hand touch the back of my neck. "Maybe this will sweeten you up," she said, and she drew in close against me.

I'd probably kissed Julie a hundred times by then, but there was something about that particular kiss that got to me. Maybe it was the warmth of her mouth in the middle of that cold, clammy rain, or the odd sensation of her soft girl's body inside that stiff, crinkly raincoat. Or maybe it was Gary's strange behavior or the fact that he was going to jail. Anyway, as Julie started to back away I sort of clutched at her, as if I couldn't bear to have her leave. At first she stiffened but then she relaxed and nestled against me.

"Good night, *mon ami*," she whispered after a moment. She stepped back and began once more to turn away, and this time I let her go. "I'll see you in the funny papers," she said.

"What about me?" Gary said.

Julie stopped. Then she turned back to look at Gary, seeming to move in slow motion.

"I need to be sweetened up, too," Gary said. "I've got a court hearing on Wednesday and I'll probably get sent to jail. That's something Wayne forgot to tell you."

Julie looked over at me but I didn't know what to say or do. I thought of laughing out loud to show that Gary was making a bad joke, or to try to turn it into one. But then I saw the expression on Gary's face and I knew I couldn't do that. It was a different expression than I'd ever seen before—sort of hopeful and alert, but frightened and defeated, too—and I knew that whatever was happening was something that was important to him. And I wondered, too, if Julie saw it, saw that raw unprotected yearning, and I hoped for Gary's sake she did.

Julie took a few slow steps in Gary's direction. She put a hand on his shoulder and looked up into his face. Her rain hood fell back and I could see her gaze moving back and forth, as though she were searching Gary's expression for something.

Suddenly she smiled. "Sure," she said, "I guess I could do that." And then she put her arms around Gary's thin shoulders and rose up on her tiptoes and started to kiss him. At first Gary just stood there, his arms hanging at his sides, but then he reached up and put his hands on her shoulders and pulled in tight against her.

After what seemed like a very long time—longer than the kiss she had given to me—Julie finally pulled away. "Good luck, *mon ami*," she said in a soft voice, and for the second time she turned away and walked back toward the house.

On the ride home Gary sat in the passenger seat, his arms folded, looking straight ahead. He seemed to have drawn back into his own private world.

"What was that all about?" I asked. For some reason my voice was shaking.

Gary stirred, as though he were waking from a dream. "What?"

"Back there. That stuff with the kiss."

He laughed a little. "It was just something I wanted to

do," he said. "Kiss a girl. Just a normal, everyday thing."

"But Julie's my girlfriend," I said.

There was a long silence. I could feel Gary watching me from across the darkened car, as if it had never occurred to him that there was anything wrong with kissing my girlfriend. As if being my brother gave him that right.

"Look at it this way, Wayne," he said, and his voice was filled with concern now, notched to a lower register. "It'll be a long time before I get to kiss another girl. Consider it a going-away gift for Gary."

We drove on for a while in silence. I was still upset, though I didn't know exactly why. Part of me had wanted Julie to kiss Gary, but part of me didn't. Then I noticed I was gripping the steering wheel very hard and I tried to make myself relax.

"Gary?" I said.

"What?"

"Why'd you take that stuff? I really want to know."

I heard him draw in a slow deep breath. When he let it out a circle of fog appeared on the windshield in front of him. Immediately it began to disappear, like a balloon losing air.

"I guess I just wanted to do something different for once," Gary said. "Do something that wasn't pre-ordained. Not be Gary for a while." I felt him look at me again. "Don't you ever feel that way, Wayne?"

I didn't answer because I knew my answer wouldn't be the one he was looking for. He and I were different people. That was something I decided in that moment.

I would never break the law, or turn myself into an-other person, or cut myself off from the people who loved me best.

Up ahead, a car slammed through a big puddle, sending up bright opposing sprays.

"You'll probably go to jail," I said.

He didn't answer me.

My parents were still out when we got home. Gary headed upstairs, and I went into the den to play records on the hi-fi set—Buddy Holly and Marvin Gaye—the songs I liked to listen to after a date. I sat alone with the lights out and the songs playing and I tried to think about Julie and feel romantic. I wanted to bring back the feeling of holding her for that moment, the feeling of being in love I guess. But I couldn't do it. The beautiful pictures I tried to build in my mind kept fading to the image of Julie in Gary's arms.

Finally I gave up. I just wanted to go to bed and forget about everything that had happened that night. I turned off the hi-fi set and headed for the stairs.

As I passed Gary's room I noticed the crack beneath the door was dark. I stopped and listened with my ear against the door, wondering what strange things he might be up to. Then I gently pushed the door open and peered inside.

At first I couldn't see anything. But then my eyes adjusted to the darkness and I saw Gary standing near the bed. In front of him were the things he'd brought home from jail—

underwear, shirts, some books, a can of shaving cream. He was moving them one by one into a canvas gym bag.

I stepped into the room and closed the door behind me. "What's going on?" I said.

"I've decided to go away for a little while, Wayne."

"Like hell you are."

Outside, the rain had stopped and the sky was clear. Moonlight streamed in through the window, casting a pearly rectangle onto the floor of Gary's room. That was the only light.

Gary finished moving the things into his gym bag. Then he took a step in my direction, stopping in the rectangle of light where I could see him better.

"I've got to get away," he said. He looked right at me.

"But why?"

He started to answer, but before he could utter a single syllable he stopped and looked helplessly around the room, as if the answer to my question lay somewhere in those shadowy spaces: in the shiny music trophies arranged in perfect rows along his bookshelves, in the posters of famous dead composers adorning his four walls, in *The Presbyterian Hymnal* sitting open on his desktop.

"Everything around here is so all-nice and perfect, Wayne," he said. "Nothing causes trouble or stinks or gets in the way." He turned to me and shrugged. "I guess I need a little less of that."

"But it doesn't make any sense," I said. "You can just go back to jail for a little while. Then it'll be all over. Like Dad said."

Gary pulled the zipper on his gym bag and I jumped at the sudden sound. "I've been reading some books," he said. "There are places I want to go. I've got a little money saved." He raised his eyes and met my stare. "Maybe I'll even get down to the coast of Mexico. There might be something there."

I looked at Gary and he looked back. And I saw the same expression I'd seen before, when he was waiting in the rain for Julie's answer, half-brazen, half-afraid, and I knew he was waiting for an answer still.

"It's crazy," I said, shaking my head.

"Maybe," Gary said. And I believe I saw him smile.

Just then I heard the sound of someone coming up the stairs. Gary heard it too. He crossed the room in two quick steps and pushed back into the closet. He pulled the door shut, although not quite all the way. Through a narrow opening I could see him standing among the hanging shirts and trousers, holding onto his gym bag, looking like a man waiting to catch a train.

The door swung open and the overhead light snapped on. "What's going on here?" my father said, although he didn't say it in a mean way.

"Nothing," I said, blinking at the sudden brightness.

"Where's Gary?"

My father's hand rested on the doorknob. He was leaning forward, as if he were about to step into the room. And I thought of the things that Gary had just told me, and I thought of what he'd said before, about not wanting to be himself anymore. And even though I couldn't make any sense of it I decided that maybe he should do that, that maybe it would be all right to try that after all.

"Gary went out for a walk," I said. "He said he wanted to think about some things." Then, as an afterthought, and because I believed it was true, I added: "I think he's scared about everything that's happening."

My father stayed rooted in the doorway, but his expression softened and his mouth curved up into a sort of knowing smile. As if he understood everything that was happening. Understood it better than we did. And for some reason that made me mad.

"Well, don't worry," he said. "Everything will work out eventually. I'm sure it will."

"I hope so, too," I said. I looked at my father and I forced myself to smile.

"Gary's got some things to learn," he continued. "It'll be hard but he'll learn them eventually."

I didn't say anything because I was still feeling that anger.

"Only I just wish he'd learn them easier." His glance moved over to a poster hanging on Gary's wall—Van Cliburn at the Russian piano festival in 1959—and his eyes narrowed a bit. "Like you," he added after a moment.

And again I didn't say anything because I didn't know what to say. But I realized I still had that smile spread across my face, a big stupid grin, as though I really wanted everything to turn out fine. But it was all a mystery to me. And I couldn't tell you exactly what I was thinking and I'm not sure I can tell you now. All I knew was that Gary was standing in the closet and my father was standing a few feet away. But they didn't know about each other, didn't know anything at all. And then I thought that maybe that's not so bad either. Maybe not knowing isn't the worst thing that can happen to people in the world.

"Why don't you go to bed, Wayne," my father said. "It's late." He stretched out his arm in my direction.

I shifted my gaze and took one last quick look at Gary. From his shadowy hiding place he looked back at me. "Okay," I said. And I turned and followed my father through the door.

I didn't know it but that was the last time I would ever see Gary. He succeeded in making his way down to the coast of Mexico, just like he said he would, to a small town in the province of Tamaulipas, although he never found the sunken treasure he was looking for. At least not as far as I knew about. By the time he came back home, one year later, I was off to college in Pennsylvania and had my own life to worry about. He stayed in town for only a few days; just long enough to have a series of increasingly bitter arguments with my father, who still held out the hope that he would one day become a famous violinist and prove those certain things about our family. And then one afternoon he disappeared again, just as he'd done before. Only this time he did not come back.

Over the years we heard different things from friends or acquaintances who claimed to know something: that

Gary had gone to Vietnam, that he was an insurance sales-man in Seattle, that he had settled down as a high school music teacher in California. But we never knew if any of it was true, and I think now that none of it was. All I know for certain is that on that night in 1964 Gary felt the need to make a choice, to change his life's easy course in some desperate and reckless way, to take control of things, even if it meant disaster—and to reach out for a source of love. And in the end I guess we are all struggling for those things, struggling for them with different skills but with the same clouded intentions. Because I know that I am struggling for them still.

After I left Gary's bedroom that night I walked down the hallway to my own room.

"Good night," my father said from the other end of the hallway.

"Good night," I said.

He flipped off the hall light and disappeared through the bedroom door.

I went into my own room. I didn't bother to get un-dressed. I just lay down on the bed. Overhead, the tangled shadows of tree branches played across the ceiling, looking like a fishnet was about to drop down on me.

There were many thoughts and feelings swirling around inside my head, but I pushed them away and forced my thoughts back onto Julie. I tried to figure out what I would say when I saw her next, how I would explain Gary's strange behavior, how I would make her like me better, how I would advance my campaign to sleep with her. And then, against my will, my thoughts turned back to Gary, and I suddenly wondered if Julie's kiss had been a factor in his decision to leave, whether it had tipped some strange internal forces out of balance, releasing pent-up passions or desire, and for some reason I found myself hoping that it had. And somewhere during all of this thinking I heard a slight noise from out in the hallway and I pictured Gary, gym bag in hand, making his way down the curving staircase and out of our house and on to the coast of Mexico, or to some other strange place that I would never know about. And then I closed my eyes and thought harder about Julie, and I tried not to think about Gary any more.

Parallel Universe

They were planning to spend the night in Savannah, find a good restaurant down by the river and see a few of the sites, when he discovered she was nearly out of oxygen. After a brief conversation in the Motel 6 parking lot, they decided to continue overnight to St. Petersburg, drive straight on through to his sister's house, where, in the front hall closet, she had left a fresh tank last May, just before boarding her flight to Michigan. Roy pictures it now—a big steel cylinder pushed back amid the off-season sweaters and his brother-in-law's hunting clothes, looking like an atom bomb or a torpedo turned up on end.

"I wonder if it will still be good?" Her wavering voice

struggles to rise above the rumbling of the nearby over-pass.

"Of course it will," Roy says. "It's not like food. It doesn't spoil. Grow bacteria." He laughs briefly. "Jesus Christ, Mom, it's oxygen. It's a chemical."

"But I wonder if it might have leaked out. Over the months. That's what I mean."

He considers this, rubs his chin. His gaze follows the clear plastic tube that curves up from the small, wheeled oxygen tank and attaches to the little device on her face. Behind the noise of the traffic Roy can detect the faint hissing sound as the device dispenses a thin stream of oxygen.

"Now that's a different matter," he says. "If it leaked out. That's a different question altogether."

They are standing at the back of her Chevrolet Impala, the brand and model of car favored by her late husband for more than twenty years. Roy ducks his head and looks down into the open trunk, takes another inventory—twelve green-painted bottles, each topped with a dial running from red to green—theoretically enough oxygen to make the trip from Michigan to Florida. The little salami-shaped tanks are stacked like cordwood between her cloth-sided suitcases and a mud-splattered spare tire. All of the dials show red.

"What about going to one of those stores?" she says. "One of those places where they refill them."

Roy emerges from the trunk. He wants nothing more than to get this trip over with. "Who knows where we'd find one," he says. "Or if it'd be open at this hour."

"Well, I'm going to walk Buddy," she says, referring to the Yorkshire terrier watching them anxiously through the rear window. "Driving on through the night may be all right for us, but Buddy needs some exercise." She starts around the side of the car, pulling the little wheeled canister as though she were leading a child by the hand.

"Wait a minute," he says. "You've got to conserve your strength. All you've got is that one bottle for the next 400 miles." He slams down the trunk. A cloud of red Georgia dust explodes upward. "Sit in the car," he says. "I'll go inside and get our money back. Then I'll walk Buddy."

They have been on the road for three days. He had started the trip with good intentions but somewhere those intentions had gotten lost. Something about their proximity in the car—mother and son—has stripped away the strained civility that had become the basis of their relationship these last few years. Things hadn't been good between them for a while. Roy hated saying it—about his own mother—but it was true.

Standing in the Motel 6 lobby waiting for the clerk to come out, Roy taps the bell and scans the bleak, no-nonsense space: the vinyl-covered chairs in two opposing rows, a corner vending machine dispensing combs, miniature tubes of toothpaste, sewing needles and thread, foil-wrapped condoms. An ancient TV, turned low, hangs from the ceiling, displaying psychedelic weather maps and a rolling strip of stock quotes.

It's early November. Back in Michigan the winds have backed around toward Manitoba and leaves are clustering in soggy heaps against fencerows and building foundations. It's well past the season for Roy's mother to be in Florida, especially with her bad heart, but this year she had not wanted to leave, had deftly parried his efforts to talk about it, seemed content to stay on in the house along the lake, devoid of neighbors since Labor Day, certainly not the place for an old lady who might need God-knows-what assistance at any moment. So finally he had forced the issue, called her late one night in a boozy, sentimental stupor and said he'd be there on a certain date, seven a.m. sharp, ready to load her things and head out.

"I'm not sure I want to go this year," she finally admitted. "I thought maybe I'd like to try to spend the winter in Michigan this year. It seems like I haven't seen a real winter since your father retired."

"Look," he said, "here's the thing, Mom. You need to be someplace where there's people around. Where there's people who can keep an eye on you."

"I suppose that makes sense," she said, hesitantly.

"Of course it does," he said. He took a swallow of his whiskey, tried to focus his thoughts. "Besides, the trip will be fun. We can stop a few places along the way. See some sights. We'll have a good time."

"Maybe we could stop one night in Savannah," she said. "I've always wanted to see Savannah."

"Sure we could," he said. "We'll put Savannah on the agenda."

"Your father," she said. "It seems like he never wanted to make any side trips. We always drove on through as fast as we could. Never left the interstate. Like we had a deadline."

Roy sipped his drink, thought about this, ten years traveling back and forth to Florida, thousands of miles, and never any side trips just for fun. His mother, he knows, would never have spoken up, would never have complained, was from that generation of women who didn't ask for much and expected less.

"Savannah," he said. "Okay. It's a deal."

In the motel lobby he taps the bell again and the receptionist comes out, a teen-age girl with a placid smile and an elaborate hairdo, probably not much older than his own daughter Allison. She smiles, places her hands on the counter. "Yes, sir," she says, stretching the word out with an extra syllable. "Is something wrong?"

Roy smiles and explains about the empty oxygen bottles, his mother with her weak heart, the big bottle—tank, actually, you would have to call it—in his sister's closet in St. Pete.

"So what we've decided to do"—he smiles crookedly, shakes his head as though what he is about to reveal defies comprehension—"what we *have* to do, actually, is to drive right on through. Through the night, I mean." The girl smiles across the counter, says nothing. "So we won't be taking the room." He places the key on the counter, pushes it in her direction. "And we'd like a refund."

❋   ❋   ❋

It was a number of things. You could take your pick. For one thing she just couldn't keep from minding everyone else's business, especially Roy's. Five years ago it had been the business with Arlene. She'd prodded him into hanging on long after it was clear to anyone with half a brain that the marriage was hopeless. That little episode was hard to forget, because the way Roy figured her meddling had cost him an extra year of misery. She'd meddled—there was no other word for it—calling Roy at his office at odd hours to ask him for an update on their latest argument, urging him to show patience and understanding, working on his guilt about leaving Allison in a broken family. Once she'd even said a prayer for their marriage, going on for several incredible minutes while Roy held the phone off and doodled on a notepad.

But nothing ever changes, nothing improves. Because it was the same thing years ago when Roy was studying the cello, when she'd badgered him into staying with it long after he knew he had no hope of turning it into a career. She'd badgered him through a music degree at Oberlin, badgered him into going off to Sioux Falls to play with the local philharmonic, badgered him into hanging on there—in Sioux Falls, for Christ's sake—even after he'd been let go, in the vain hope that another position would open up.

Roy walks back to the car, the cancelled receipt in his hand. He thinks about his life. At forty-three he builds small subdivisions in the farm fields around Grand Rapids, what could charitably be called tract housing, small, low-slung ranchettes with vinyl siding, gravel driveways, transplanted silver maples yellowing in the front yards. It provides him a livelihood—that was what he used to say to Arlene—perhaps not such a bad ending for someone who'd thrown away so many fine young years.

He reaches the car and sees that it's empty. He turns and scans the parking lot. In the distance, toward the overpass, he sees his mother making her ragged way across a field of weeds and stacks of plywood, holding Buddy's leash with one hand and pulling along the little tethered canister with the other, stopping now and giving a tug to free the wheels from the soft sandy soil.

Roy jogs over to her. "Mom, what're you doing?"

"Buddy got restless." She gives another tug on the oxygen tank to move it through the soft soil.

"Here," Roy says, reaching for the leash. "For Christ's sake, Mom."

She opens her hand, surrenders the little strip of leather. "Please don't talk that way, Roy. You know I don't like it when you take the Lord's name in vain."

He ignores her and reaches for the canister, closes his hand around hers that feels startlingly devoid of flesh. He notices that her breathing is shallow and quick.

"Can you make it back to the car, Mom? Maybe we should just stand here for a moment and rest."

"I'm all right," she says. But he hears the quaver in her voice, and when she takes a half step forward she stops, her shoes sunk a good two inches in the sand. There is a slight tremble in her arm.

"Just wait," he says. He lets go of the tank and wraps his hand onto her upper arm, lifts slightly, steadies her. "Just wait here and catch your breath," he says.

They stand for several minutes, her breath coming in little puffs. He is conscious of the thinness of her arm, the overall sense of frailness, of impending calamity. Above them, sixteen-wheeled tractor-trailers boom on the overpass, sending down a torrent of noise and faint emanations of diesel fumes. Slowly her breathing deepens, evens out, and the slight tremble in her arm disappears.

"Are you all right now?" he says. "Can you make it back to the car?"

"Of course I can," she says. She pulls her arm free of his grasp, steps forward, taking high steps in the sandy soil.

On the road now, the setting sun a pyrotechnics show through her side window.

"Isn't that beautiful?" she says. But not like it's a question; not like it's even addressed to anyone. Just a thought.

He glances over, registers a split second's worth of mottled reds, oranges, golds, brings his eyes back onto the thrumming road ahead.

"Sure is," he says.

A red convertible comes up behind them, grows enormous in the rear view mirror, veers left and thunders past. Inside is a leather-jacketed man and a woman with giant sunglasses, her blond hair whipping madly in the wind. For a moment Roy imagines himself in that car, a pretty girl at his side, an hour or two away from a quiet room, a few drinks, a shared bed. It's been five months since he broke up with his latest girlfriend, Laura. He feels the absence of love in his life, considers for a moment, and decides he should do something about it when he gets back to Grand Rapids.

He glances down at the oxygen tank, which with Buddy is sharing the empty space between them. The needle hovers around the middle of the dial, in the vast no-man's land between the red and the green zones. It occurs to Roy for the first time that perhaps their predicament is more serious than he's thought, that instead of St. Petersburg they should be heading straight for the nearest hospital.

"What happens if it runs dry?"

"Runs dry?" She repeats the words in a croaky voice, not understanding.

He flicks his glance down to the bottle, then back onto the road. "The oxygen," he says. "What if it runs out before we get to St. Petersburg?"

She scratches Buddy behind the ears; the dog emits a low groan and rolls onto his side. "It just runs out," she says.

"But what about you? That's what I mean. What'll happen to you?"

"I guess I'll be all right. As long as I'm not running in any races or climbing any mountains."

"You're sure?" he says.

She turns her head away, looks back out at the sky, the brilliant colors now edged with grays and blacks. From Roy's angle, her head looks sunk between her shoulders. There is no clear sense of where her body ends and her head begins. It's as if everything is collapsing in on itself, which, he thinks, in a way, it is.

"As sure as I can be about anything," she answers finally.

Dark now, the traffic thinned out, through the windshield billboards looming up announcing praline shacks and antebellum theme parks, civil war battlefields. He glances over. His mother and Buddy are asleep. The instrument panel throws a greenish glow onto her fingers twined in Buddy's mottled fur. Her head is tilted at an odd angle against the seat back. He hears the gentle hiss of the oxygen.

He is tired, his eyes heavy, his thoughts loose and drifty. His mind skims randomly over the landscape of his life, then settles on an incident from 1961, when he was nine, the year they moved to his father's big new job in Flint, a bleak company town bristling with labor strife. There was a large new house, a certain amount of social standing, more money and the things that money buys. And then suddenly, without explanation, his mother had disappeared, went off to live with her sister in Chicago. Roy tries to remember how long she had been gone; was it three weeks or four? Anyway, he remembers the odd, preoccupied behavior of his father and the letters that came at irregular intervals, a page or two in her cramped up-and-down hand, the tone vague and slightly flippant, seeming, really, to have been composed by some other person than his mother, going on about the fascinating things she was doing in Chicago: the trips to the symphony, the parks along Lake Michigan, her excursions to art museums, the neighborhood where her sister lived, filled with masterpieces by Frank Lloyd Wright.

A semi truck comes up behind them. Roy watches it in the rear-view mirror. As it cannonballs past there is a moment of sparkling blindness, its headlights shooting back into Roy's eyes, crazy refractions dancing across the grimy, bug-encrusted windshield.

Roy settles back again, relaxes. After a moment, he becomes aware that his mother is awake. Her head is resting against the seat back but her eyes are open. Her fingers are slowly working Buddy's fur.

"Mom," he says, "do you remember that time in Flint when you went to visit Aunt Harriet for a few weeks?" His voice in the quiet of the car startles him, sounding too loud.

"Yes, I remember."

"Well, what was that all about? I've always wondered."

"I don't know what you mean."

"You left so suddenly. We'd barely moved into the new house. And then you came back later as if nothing had happened."

For a while she is quiet. "I thought you knew," she finally says.

"What?" he says.

"Your father and I," she says, "we had some troubles then. We had things to work out. I did, anyway."

He rubs his eyes, works his jaw back and forth, can't believe what he has just heard.

"We were different, your father and I," she goes on. "In certain ways we were very different. I guess that's what it came down to."

Several minutes pass. He thinks she may have drifted off to sleep again. But then she speaks, her voice soft and a little husky. "But we stayed together. I think it was the right decision. Don't you?"

A rest stop outside Jacksonville, acres of empty asphalt dotted with streetlights, in back a small army of trucks angled into parking spaces abutting a forest of pine trees. Roy walks Buddy over to the grassy fringe, stands while the little dog raises a rear leg and pees in a series of nervous spurts.

He tries to make sense of what he has just learned. The idea of his mother leaving his father is as incredible to him as space aliens. It defies everything he has believed about her, her old practiced role as a sort of affable and easily overlooked accessory to his father's life. Then he tries to imagine what his own life would be like if she had not come back, how things might have played out differently. But the vision breaks down before he can carry it very far forward; it's like an alternate reality, one of those parallel universes that you read about in science fiction, existing in the fissures of the real world.

"So what brought you back?" he asks her, when he has returned to the car. "From Chicago that time." He holds the passenger-side door open. Buddy jumps up onto her lap.

"You did," she says. She scratches Buddy's ears. "I had to take care of you."

He closes the door and walks around the car. "That's perfect," he says, but not so she can hear him.

The middle of the night. A Mobil station somewhere near Ocala. Rows of mercury lights beam down like spotlights on a movie set. Roy replaces the hose on the pump, retrieves his credit card from the machine. Inside the building a Dunkin' Donuts counter shares space with shelves of brake fluid, lubricating oil, gallon jugs of Coke on sale for $1.19.

"I'm going to get a cup of coffee," he tells her.

"Wait a minute," she says. "I'll come with you." She opens the side door, slowly brings her legs around, grips the seatback, pauses before pushing herself upright. Roy comes over and takes her arm. The oxygen tank, its dial pointing to the red zone, stays behind.

Inside, an attendant—a large girl with spiky hair—comes out from behind a Plexiglas panel and serves them coffee and glazed donuts. She smiles, asks where they're from, where they're headed, then goes back behind the

Plexiglas and picks up a paperback. Mother and son sit in a booth and sip their coffee.

"How is Laura these days?" she asks him. "You haven't said anything about Laura for a while."

Roy bristles at the question, knows he has answered it before. "Laura and I decided to go our separate ways, Mom. You remember. It happened a few months ago."

"That's too bad," she says.

"It was for the best."

They sit for a while in silence. "Maybe your standards are too high, Roy," she says. "Maybe you expect too much from people."

He ignores her, looks out the window.

"In my generation men and women were more forgiving. We expected less. I guess there's nothing wrong with that."

Outside, a battered pick-up rolls up to the gas island. A teen-aged boy gets out and begins to work the pump. After a moment his girlfriend, a skinny blond in jeans and tee-shirt, comes over and embraces him, lets her head rest tiredly against his shoulder. They make an odd tableau— teen-age lovers gassing up a pick-up in the middle of the night—which, for some reason, touches Roy deeply.

"Do you ever play the cello anymore, Roy?" his mother says. "I wonder about that from time to time."

"No, Mom," he says, wearily, turning back to her. "That's ancient history."

"Never?" she says.

"Nope. Never ever."

She picks up a spoon and begins to stir her coffee. "That's a shame. You were so good at it."

"Not good enough," he says. He looks back out the window.

"I don't know about that," she says. "I think you gave it up too soon."

Roy's mind, stupid with fatigue and days of being on the road, begins to fill with a diffuse anger. The absurdity of the situation strikes him with a certain pathetic force, mother and son sitting in a broken-down gas station at 3:00 a.m., picking up the threads of a disagreement that is decades old.

"Give it up, Mom," he says, a little too loud. "It's over and done with."

Behind the Plexiglas, the girl looks up from her paperback. Roy shoots her a glance and she lowers her head.

He leans across the table. "Anyway, you had your chance about that years ago, if you remember."

Roy's mother returns his stare with a calmness that surprises him. For a moment he wonders if she has heard him—and then, crazily, if he has actually spoken words or just imagined them.

She wets her finger, picks a crumb up off the table, flicks it onto the floor.

"I know it's not my business," she says, finally. "But I always thought you had a talent. You played so beautifully, Roy. It broke my heart when you came back from Sioux Falls that last time."

He can't believe what he is hearing. It's all so crazy.

Twenty years ago. He rubs his temples, tries to staunch the rage that is building in him. All the disappointments of a lifetime seem to be occupying the space with him in this booth.

He begins to talk. "The way I figured it, Mom, is that you're a good part of the reason things turned out the way they did." He spits the words out, low and vicious. "If you hadn't been pushing so hard, always talking about how great I was, what a brilliant future I had......" He leaves the thought unfinished.

Roy's mom looks off to the side, then back at Roy, blinks, looks off again. A moment passes, and then Roy is aware of the girl standing next to their booth. "Refill?" she asks brightly.

Roy looks up at the girl. She is holding a steaming pot of coffee. On her wrist he sees a tattoo, some kind of bird or exotic sea creature. "No, thanks," he says.

The girl turns to Roy's mother, who is still looking off to the side. "Refill?" she repeats.

Roy's mother does not respond. There is an awkward, stretching silence. The girl glances at Roy, looks back at Roy's mom, then lifts the pot and tilts her head inquiringly. Roy remembers the green canister in the car, wonders if his mother has fallen into some kind of oxygen-deprived state, wonders whether anything is registering with her at all.

He leans forward and touches her arm. "Mom," he says.

At first she doesn't move. But then she brings her gaze around and her eyes lock onto Roy's. It's only a moment, but long enough for him to see the fury there, the hard-etched wrinkles, a deep-burning rage, although whether it is directed at him or at herself he cannot say.

He lets go of her arm and draws his hand back, as if repelled by some invisible force. He watches as her shoulders rise and fall, rise and fall again. Finally she turns and smiles up at the girl. "I will have just a little more coffee, thank you."

The girl bobs her spiked head, gives a relieved smile, begins to pour a stream of coffee into the white mug.

"That's a beautiful tattoo you have there," the old woman says. "A butterfly."

The girl smiles with pleasure. "Thanks," she says. "I got it just last week."

They are finished with their coffee. Roy helps his mother out to the car. He supports her as they make their slow way under the blaze of mercury lights. Opening the car door, he holds her hands as she backs down into the seat, then he helps her work her legs around. Before closing the door he leans across and examines the oxygen bottle, notices that the needle is not quite all the way through the red zone.

"There's a little bit left in here, Mom," he says. "I'm going to hook it up." Still leaning in, he busies himself with the plastic tube, arranges the device on her face, then gives a half turn to the silver handle on top of the green tank. He hears the slow, steady hiss as the gas begins flowing.

"See, it's not finished yet," he tells her. "I bet there's enough to make it." He shifts his gaze and looks at her. Her bright eyes stare back, unblinking. He's aware of the nearness of their faces.

"Thank you," she says.

He closes her door and begins to walk around the car. But then he stops and leans back against the fender. For a moment he stares off, remembering her fierce expression inside the station, and he thinks again about her going off that time in '61—her one desperate grab—and then returning. And then he thinks about his own life's course and wonders if she could be right, if perhaps he had been destined for better things, and if better things were still not possible for him, even now.

He smiles and shakes his head, decides he will think about it later, when his mind is clear. He opens the door and slides his body under the steering wheel, then looks out though the streaked windshield. In front of him, just beyond the bright cascade of mercury lights, a field of corn rises up against the asphalt parking lot. The coarse green stalks lead off in endless rows that look like ocean waves. Roy squints, trying to see them better.

The Five O'Clock Train

In Paris they stayed in a small third-floor apartment in the Seventh District not far from Napoleon's Tomb. There was a market two blocks away where they went in the morning for cheese and croissants. Afterwards, they walked back to their apartment holding hands and carrying their bags of groceries and the *Herald Tribune* and feeling a little like they belonged there, like they were Parisians, or at least like they thought Parisians should feel.

During the day they visited parks and museums and tried to find the old special places they remembered from their honeymoon. Each evening they dined at a different restaurant in their neighborhood. It was always a different restaurant and it was always in their neighborhood. For some reason, taking their meals in the local places made them feel a little less like tourists.

On Wednesday of the second week they stopped at noon in a café on the Boulevard Saint-Germain. They had walked over from their neighborhood and they were quite tired. It was a sunny day and the boulevard was filled with pedestrians and the traffic in the street was very heavy. In front of them, Citrones and Peugeots inched forward in a jerky, stop-and-go fashion.

"Have you noticed," said Peter, "how rarely Parisian drivers use their horns."

"I think it's because of their innate respect for their fellow man," said Eleanor.

"Do you think so?" He looked at her. He could never tell when she was serious.

Eleanor saw him looking and smiled. "Maybe it would be good to leave the city for a day," she said. "We could get away from the crowds and the noise. See a little of the countryside."

"Where can we go?"

Eleanor sipped her drink. "Let's go to Auvers," she said.

"Where?"

"Auvers. It's a small village just outside Paris where Van Gogh and some other French painters used to spend time. Van Gogh actually died there, as a matter of fact. You know Van Gogh."

"Of course I know Van Gogh. He cut off his ear."

"Bravo," Eleanor said, raising her glass in a mock salute.

"And he did some other interesting things too."

Peter smiled, although he didn't like the tone of Eleanor's voice. Perhaps he imagined it, but it seemed like he detected a little trace of malice, like back in Chicago.

They had met six years earlier when she was finishing work on her Master of Fine Arts degree at the University of Chicago. Peter, a junior stockbroker struggling to build a stable of clients, was a little unclear about what the term "Fine Arts" actually meant, and on their second date he asked her.

"It means 'art,'" she said. "You know: painting, sculpture, that sort of thing." Under her breath she added something that Peter did not quite catch.

They were walking along the breakwater in front of the aquarium by Grant Park. Peter stopped and rested his elbows on a concrete pier and looked out onto Lake Michigan. It was July. A flock of sea gulls dipped and soared out over the water.

"Oh," he said. " I thought that maybe 'fine arts' meant something different from, you know, just art."

Eleanor cocked her head and gave him an appraising, squinty-eyed look. "Are you serious?" she asked him.

He turned and looked at her. "About what?" he said.

She continued looking at him. Then she smiled and shook her head.

She wasn't what you would call a beauty but there was a quality about her that was striking, something that made

Peter want to look at her, not in awe but with a sense of interest and respect. She was tall and thin and pale, and she moved delicately and deliberately, like a cat. Her long auburn hair was often piled loosely on her head in a formless, tangled mass, a few wayward strands hanging down and giving her the look of a slightly harried librarian. Her hands were like delicate instruments; they always seemed to be in motion, clutching at the air as if she were trying to grasp ideas and give them form. Often, they carried the stains of paints and lacquers.

But it was her personality that captivated Peter most. He found her mysterious and unfathomable, like a visitor from some exotic country. When she talked about her art he listened with a rapt, childlike attention. Her world of form and color and composition was to him an alien territory: as far as he was concerned she might as well be talking about the marriage customs of some African tribe, or the politics of Eskimos. And when she finished one of her elaborate and energetic discourses—about the importance of "line" in Manet's "The Dead Toreador," say, or the "resonances" of Cezanne's colors—he would clap his hands and howl, not because he understood her, because he did not, but because she was so sincerely enthusiastic about something that was, to him, implausible and absurd.

Once she had told him she could feel some works of art in her body.

"I don't believe you."

"It's true. It's like a physical sensation. I swear it."

"What does it feel like?"

She pursed her lips in a parody of deep thought. "Sometimes it's like a little caress across my shoulders, and sometimes it's like a draught from a window, and sometimes it's like someone has slapped me across the face. Some of Matisse's works make me feel that way."

"You're teasing me now," he said. "This is a joke."

She took his hand and did a sort of pirouette, laughing. "You'll never know, mister stockbroker," she said. "You'll never know."

But he loved her. Or at least he thought he did. Insofar as he understood what love was all about. To him, she was like a medium who could commune with a parallel world, or a brilliant physicist who understood the time and space continuum, or a holy man who glimpses into the mind of God. There is, she seemed to be telling him, another world out there. And perhaps—just perhaps—it is a better world than the one you know.

But now it was the fifth year of their marriage and something seemed to have changed. In the evening they talked less about the little adventures of the day and, when they did, the conversation had a distracted, desultory tone, as if each of them were thinking of something else. More importantly, they had begun to argue with a new fervor. It was a small change, a barely perceptible uptick in the volume and intensity of their disagreements, as if an ugly yellow vein of malice had secretly found its way into the bedrock of their marriage. They had always been at odds about many things, but in the past their arguments had been benign and even humorous events. Their voices in combat had carried a false note, a slight and inappropriate amplification, almost like they were playing to an invisible audience.

But now all that had changed. The situation reached a crisis of sorts one Sunday afternoon in early October. They were walking their basset Bruce in an open field near their home. Bruce had been having accidents lately that were playing havoc with the carpets and as they walked along Peter enumerated the reasons why it would be best for everyone, Bruce included, if the dog were put down. As he spoke he counted off his points on his fingers, a bit of showmanship that Eleanor did not appreciate. Bruce had been her dog since before they had been married and the thought of parting with him at this vulnerable stage was heartbreaking.

Peter drew to a close: "We just can't continue like this, Elly. We've got too much invested in the house and the furnishings to let it be jeopardized by an old, incontinent dog. It's the sensible thing to do. You'll see."

Eleanor knelt down and began to scratch Bruce behind his ears. The old dog looked up at her with a mournfulness that was, in its own preposterous way, exquisite. His tail pulsed back and forth like a metronome. Eleanor bent her head so that her long hair fell around the dog's knobby skull. She scratched his velvety ears. "You're such a nice dog, Bruce," she murmured from inside the little tent of hair. "You're so loyal and kind."

She bent and kissed Bruce on the top of his head, letting her lips linger against his rough fur for a long moment. And then with a weary sigh she pushed herself upright and looked at Peter. There was a pause, like the moment when a high diver has flexed the board and is waiting to be catapulted into space. "And you, Peter," she said in a quiet voice, "can go straight to hell." And then she took the leash from Peter's hand and turned and walked in the direction of their house, alone.

The next day she called him at his office.

"I'm going to buy some airline tickets to Paris for the first two weeks of November," she said.

"What are you talking about?" said Peter. His mind had been on a listing of stock quotes.

"We're going to Paris. It'll be like a second honeymoon. We need to do this. Things are getting out of control. Things between us, I mean." There was a pause. "Just shut up and clear your calendar." And then she hung up.

Peter put down the receiver and leaned back in his chair. A little smile came onto his face. There had been a tone in Eleanor's voice, a tone that he remembered. A sort of exuberant quality that he had not heard for a long time.

Now they walked up from the train station along the dusty street of the ancient French village to the inn where

Van Gogh had died. The building had been restored and the new owners had mounted polished brass plaques along the walls of the courtyard explaining notable events in the painter's life and the circumstances of his death. On the top floor of the inn there was a small room with a skylight and a bed and a single wooden chair and a plaque on the wall explaining that this was the room where the painter had died.

"So he shot himself and it took him two days to die," said Peter.

"Evidently," said Eleanor. She leaned over the roped barrier to peer into the dim interior.

"Jeez," said Peter.

Outside, the sun was shining brightly. It was warm and they carried their jackets slung over their shoulders. Peter didn't notice any other tourists in the village. Evidently, this was not such a popular attraction after all, he thought. As they walked along the dusty streets, they followed a map they had picked up at the train station. The map gave the locations of the scenes that Van Gogh had painted during the final furious weeks of his life. It showed the famous wooden stairway that went to the upper part of the village, and the riverbank with boats, and the wheat field with the flight of crows.

"This place is a little creepy," said Peter. "Everything you see reminds you of a dead painter." They were on the upper part of the village passing a house that was being restored by a group of workmen. The stones that formed the walls had been taken down and stacked carefully along the street and the heavy, rough timbers that framed the house were exposed. Peter noticed that the stones had been marked with daubs of red paint to show how they went back together. He stopped to examine them, trying to figure out the code.

"What do you mean?" Eleanor said, stopping too.

"I can't explain it," he said. "I just have this eerie feeling."

They walked along a little further. "I don't think it's eerie," she said. "I think it's very spiritual. Van Gogh was so close to death but all he could do was paint. It's like he was under some compulsion to make a record of the world just before he was going to leave it."

"I suppose so," said Peter.

"It's almost like the act of painting *was* his life," she continued. "His essence, I mean. And once it was finished his corporal existence didn't matter any more."

Peter looked over at his wife. She was staring straight ahead, her gaze fixed on the far horizon. It irritated him when she made these grandiose statements. He knew it shouldn't but it did.

"That's a little too philosophical for me," he said.

They walked along the upper street of the town. Peter noticed that many of the old houses had been restored. They all seemed to have new mortar between the ancient stones.

"It must cost a fortune to fix up one of these old buildings," he volunteered.

"I suppose so," said Eleanor.

❋   ❋   ❋

Later, they sat on the terrace of a café along the main street of the village. The café was next to the train station. There were tiny folding chairs with white wooden slats clustered around wrought iron tables. The tables were protected from the sun by yellow umbrellas. A series of train tracks ran behind the café and every few minutes they heard the hiss of the air brakes on one of the trains.

An elderly waiter came out onto the terrace and took their order. He walked with great deliberation, like he was suffering from some painful joint disease. After he took their order he bowed and backed away.

"Maybe he's one of Vincent's old buddies," Peter said.

"What?"

"Maybe our waiter knew Van Gogh. He looks like he might have been around back then."

Eleanor smiled thinly. "I don't think so. That would make him about a hundred and twenty."

"You never know."

The old waiter reappeared with two glasses on a copper tray. He placed the glasses carefully on paper coasters. Little beads of moisture coated the glasses.

"You look very thoughtful," Peter said.

"I was just thinking about how happy I am right now. I feel so fortunate to be here." She smiled happily. "I suppose it's hard for you to understand how much all this means to me."

Peter said nothing.

"Because to an artist this is a sacred place," she continued. "An artistic miracle took place here. And it's so poignant and sad because of the way it happened. Van Gogh destroyed himself. He drove himself mad from his urge to capture the world in his art." Her hands fluttered for a moment in the air, as if she wanted to make a gesture and then changed her mind. She gave a quick embarrassed laugh.

Peter sipped his drink. He didn't know what to say. This kind of talk always made him uneasy.

He cleared his throat. Looking into his drink he said, "Although I read in the brochure that it could have been epilepsy."

"What?" Eleanor said. She said it like she was coming back from being a long way away.

"Epilepsy," Peter repeated in a louder voice. "Doctors who've read the accounts of Van Gogh's behavior think he may have been suffering from epileptic seizures. It probably wasn't insanity at all. It was a medical condition." Eleanor looked across the table at Peter. She had a funny expression on her face. Her eyes were etched by a series of tiny lines as though she were looking into a bright light, or was in pain. It reminded Peter of how she'd looked one time when they had seen the mutilated body of a dead cat along the side of a highway.

Eleanor picked up a straw and began to stir her drink. "Sometimes I wonder if we even understand each other any more," she said. There was a slightly clipped, nervous quality to her voice.

"What are you talking about?" said Peter. He had lifted his glass but then set it down without taking a drink.

"I wonder whether we're able to communicate about certain things. We're so different."

What the hell, thought Peter. He reached across and took her hand. "Of course we can communicate, Elly. Didn't we communicate yesterday when we decided to come here for the day? And haven't we been communicating all week in Paris? It's been great, Eleanor. You know it's been great."

"But this place," she said, and this time she made a gesture that seemed to include it all. "I don't think you're enjoying yourself. You think it's creepy. That's what you said."

"Yes, I did say that. But that doesn't mean I'm not enjoying myself. In fact, I think that's part of the charm." He cast about wildly for an idea. He had the feeling that something was slipping away. "I mean, to think of Van Gogh walking around here and painting everything he sees, and then he shoots himself. That's very moving."

She looked across the table with a sad smile. "I have an idea," she said. "Why don't you stay here and have another drink and I'll walk up to the cemetery. That's the last thing I want to see and it'll only take a few minutes."

"But I'd be glad to come along," he said.

"I know you would, sweetheart," she said. "But I'd sort of like to go alone."

She began to gather up her things. "You're very sweet," she said, unaccountably.

He watched her walk away. Halfway across the street she turned and flashed him an earnest, reassuring smile.

It was four-thirty and the train was due in half an hour. Peter looked around for the waiter but he seemed to have disappeared. He slipped a fifty-franc bill from his wallet and set it on the table, pinning it down with an ashtray so the breeze would not blow it away. Fifty francs was far too much but he couldn't wait any longer.

He started walking in the direction of the cemetery. The breeze blowing up from the river stirred up whirling clouds of dust that appeared and disappeared in the street like ghosts. Peter closed his eyes and turned his head, following the little dancing clouds.

When he reached the upper level of the village he was breathing hard and he could feel his heart pounding in his chest. He was a little light-headed. He'd drunk more than he should have. He'd told himself he wasn't going to drink much but he'd done it anyway. It was because he'd been upset by their conversation. He was upset by the way the whole day was going. He sensed that they were drifting away from each other again. All the problems from Chicago were coming back.

Next to the road a small sign on a stake announced "Tombe d'artist," with an arrow pointing ahead. The road passed the medieval church they had seen earlier in the day. It rose up at the crest of the hill like a fortress. Peter remembered that it had been the subject of one of the artist's most famous paintings.

He stopped for a moment to catch his breath. He had the odd sense of things becoming blurry at the edges. Perhaps it's all for the best, he thought blurrily. Perhaps it was time to be sensible. Perhaps he and Eleanor were just too different to be together. They were both fine people in their own way but perhaps they were just too different to live together as man and wife. He was pretty sure that Eleanor was beginning to believe that too. That was what she had meant in the café about not understanding each other.

Beyond the church the road became even narrower and rose up gradually. There were open fields on both sides of the road and when Peter turned around he could see the red-tiled rooftops of the village. Starting to walk again, he saw up ahead the white stone walls of the cemetery. It appeared starkly in an open, treeless field. He knew he would find Eleanor there, probably standing next to the artist's grave, lost in some kind of reverie.

As he came nearer he spotted an older, white-haired woman sitting in front of an easel on a little folding chair. Eleanor was standing next to her. The woman had set up her easel next to the road and she was painting the view of the countryside. Eleanor and the woman were talking. As he approached, he could see that the woman was upset about something.

"But I don't see what business it is of yours," the woman was saying to Eleanor. "It's my affair entirely." From the way she talked Peter could tell she was an American.

"I understand that," Eleanor said. "But it's just not a good idea. I think you'll agree after you've had a chance to think about it."

The woman stared at Eleanor. She looked a little frightened. "Leave me alone," she said.

"But don't you understand," said Eleanor. "It's pointless to paint a subject that another artist has used, unless it means something to you. You should find your own subject and interpret it in your own way."

The woman turned back to her painting and made a stab at the canvas with her brush. "If I want to paint the same subject that's my business. I'm not bothering you."

Peter came up next to Eleanor and touched her arm. When she looked at him he could tell she had been crying. He was quite sure that seeing Van Gogh's grave had made her cry.

"We've got to get to the train station, Elly," he said quietly.

Without speaking, she turned and started walking in the direction of the village. He could tell that she was very stirred up about something. After a moment she said: "That woman was painting the wheat field."

Peter did not understand what she meant and so he said nothing.

"It's such a desecration to his memory," she continued. "They shouldn't allow people to do that. Don't you agree?" She reached out and grasped his wrist. "They shouldn't let them come on their stupid tours and set up their little easels and pretend that they know anything about painting or art." She stopped walking and looked at him. They were standing in front of the old church. It rose up mutely in the warm afternoon sun. "When Van Gogh painted that field it meant everything in the world to him," she said. "Trying to get it down on canvas drove him crazy. But to that woman it's just an amusement. It's something she can tell her friends about back in Cleveland, or Seattle, or wherever the hell she comes from. Can't you just hear her? 'Here's the wheat field that Van Gogh painted just before he killed himself.' Then they'll all move on to the bridge table, or to the patio for cocktails."

She had finished talking now and Peter could tell. He knew that she was very stirred up about something but he didn't know exactly why and he didn't know what to say or do. He tried hard to concentrate through the blurry feeling the drinks had left behind. Turning away, he looked out over the countryside where he saw a river meandering in graceful brown curves across the green landscape and, beyond that, the smokestacks of a factory. He did not understand what Eleanor was talking about but he understood that she was very stirred up. That was very clear. And he understood that she was frightened. And he understood that he could help.

"You're entirely right," he murmured, almost to himself.

"What?" she said.

"You're right," he said again, more loudly. He dropped his gaze and shook his head slowly back and forth, as if the madness of the world defied his comprehension. "It doesn't make any sense at all. They shouldn't allow those things to happen."

Eleanor leaned forward and studied his face with an anxious searching expression. She looked at him for a very long time. And then she smiled faintly and took his hand and raised it to her face, tilted her cheek into the perfect, supplicating curve of his palm, and he felt the hot flush on her cheek from when she had been crying.

After a moment they continued walking in the direction of the train station. They arrived just in time to catch the five o'clock train. The next day in Paris they visited the last of the special places and on Saturday they flew home.

Family Way

In the evenings my father quizzed me. Standing at the kitchen sink with his hands in soapy dishwater, the sleeves of his white shirt turned up above his elbows, he would ask me to explain the principals of science and mathematics and history that I had learned that day at school. A good recital earned a brief smile and a stiff nod of his head. But if an answer was sloppy, or I acted disinterested, or sullen, he would cross-examine me until the poverty of my knowledge was exposed, and then tell me to prepare a better explanation for the next evening.

"I understand that you've memorized the Gettysburg address, Danny," he said to me one night. "But tell me its significance. It was more than a bunch of high-sounding words. Lincoln had a practical purpose in mind."

This was in the fall of 1957, the year I turned twelve, the year the Russians sent their Sputnik into outer space and proved that they were way ahead of us. My father and I were living in a rented cabin on a lake in northern Michigan, nine miles out from the little town of Meridith. The previous winter he had left his foreman's job in a General Motors' factory in Grand Rapids to take over a sales territory for a company that made power hand tools. Being a salesman was a new career for him, but he understood tools and how to work with your hands and he believed that explaining things to people—explaining good products that were durable and well manufactured—was all you needed for success. Selling, he'd told my mother the previous December when he announced his brave plans to her, was the perfect outlet for his talents, and he believed that he would make a great deal of money doing it, and we would see big improvements in our lives.

He handed me a plate. I held it under the running faucet. "I guess it meant the country was going forward with the Civil War," I answered. "There would be no turning back."

"That's part of it," he said. "But what else?"

I let a long silence fill the room, knowing that my failure to supply a ready answer—blunt proof that I was not the budding genius he wanted me to be—would irritate him. After a moment he glanced in my direction.

"It meant that we were all the same country," I said. "We had to stay together, even if it caused a lot of pain."

He grunted impatiently, then pinched a burning cigarette off the counter's edge and took a deep drag. He was silent for a long time, staring out the window at the lake glistening in the setting sun, and I thought that my answer must have dislodged some vagrant fact that needed a moment's reflection. My father was not well educated but he liked to read and he had read many books about Lincoln. Possibly he identified with the rail-splitter President: his struggle to transform himself from a backwoods bumpkin into a pillar of society; his problematic marriage; the bad luck that haunted him throughout his life.

"Okay, Danny, but what about the Negro?" He set the cigarette back on the counter, his wet fingers leaving a mark where they had touched the paper. His hands went back into the dishwater. "What was the black man's role in all this violence?"

I thought about his question but it made no sense. The word Negro didn't even appear in the Gettysburg address and I told him so.

"Well that's a question you need to think about, then," he said. "Just because something isn't mentioned doesn't mean it's not there. See if you can find an answer and we'll talk about it tomorrow."

My father believed in the infinite possibilities of self-improvement. *His* father had been a Dutch immigrant who had worked all his life as a house painter. When they opened the General Motors factory in Grand Rapids my father had gotten a job on the production line, and in time he had made it into the tool-and-die trade, which he was good at, and then into the lower ranks of management. But his real love was the outdoors. He'd learned to hunt and to fish during the Depression from a man named Harry Sherwood, an elder in the Reformed Church, and he loved those things still, loved the freedom they conveyed, the sense of possibilities. Living on a lake was his idea of the perfect place for us, even though the weather turned cold after Labor Day and most of the other cottages stood boarded-up and empty. But for me it was different: I rode a bus to school in Meridith, a town of rundown stores and empty grain elevators, and attended classes with the children of lumberjacks and farm hands. Afternoons I spent countless hours alone, casting for bass from the end of a rickety wooden dock or reading books about the military academy at West Point, where I wanted to be a cadet one day.

"I've got to drive to Grayling tomorrow," my father said now. He had drained the sink and was putting away the dishes I had just dried. "There's a man in the Western Auto there who wants to talk about moving his account over to us. It ought to be an easy sale, if my instincts are good for anything."

He looked at me as if he expected a response, some affirmation or encouragement. But this time it was my turn to give a grunting, inarticulate reply. I was tired of the games he played to keep alive the fiction that everything was fine. Six months into his new career I knew that he was failing. I'd seen the letters on a closet shelf demanding back rent on the cabin, and I'd heard his late-night telephone calls to my Uncle Glenn in Lansing, asking for a loan. Three weeks ago my mother had reached her limit. She'd gone off to live at her parents' house in Boca Raton, Florida, explaining that she needed a respite from the pioneering style of life. It was hard for me to blame her. The little summer cottage we lived in was cramped and smelled of mildew. The only heat came from a kerosene stove that you lit each morning with a wooden match. On nights when the wind blew up from the lake you could feel the walls shake and watch the curtains tremble like restless ghosts around the window frames. Worst of all there seemed to be no end in sight. The blueprints for the house my father intended to build in town—a brick ranch style that he and my mother had selected one high-spirited night from a *Good Housekeeping* magazine—lay neglected in a drawer.

"I talked to your mother this afternoon on the phone," my father said now. I set a plate onto the drain board and turned and looked out the window where a gray heron was wading in the reeds along the lakeshore.

"Is she coming back soon?" I said

"I don't know. She didn't say."

"Didn't you ask her?"

"I did. But she didn't favor me with a response."

The heron lifted a leg and planted it slowly out in front, pausing to detect some movement in the water.

"Is she mad?"

"I don't know. She's not mad at you. She may be mad at me."

He took a jar of instant coffee from the cupboard and measured a spoonful into a mug. Then he carried the mug over to the stove and added some water from a steaming kettle.

"Why is she mad at you?"

"For leaving my job with General Motors, I suppose, and casting my lot with the minions of the highway. I guess she doesn't like my new profession."

I didn't know what minions-of-the-highway meant, but I knew that my mother had not wanted my father to leave his job with General Motors. *Her* father had been the comptroller for the Hudson Vacuum Cleaner Company in Chicago and as a girl she'd known a comfortable life, even during the Depression years. She understood the advantages that came from working for a large corporation and she assumed that my father would follow that path. In the months before we left Grand Rapids to join my father in Meridith she'd taken to her bed with terrible headaches. More than once I'd missed a day of school to stay home and take care of her, reading to her from the poetry books that she loved, and boiling water on the stove to make hot compresses that she held against her forehead.

"She's going to call back later tonight," my father said now. "She wants to talk to you."

"About what?"

"Just to say hi, I imagine." He sat down at the kitchen table and placed the mug of coffee on the oilskin table-cloth. "And to remind you that she loves you. She said she's afraid you'll forget that important fact if it's left unspoken for too long."

"I know that she loves me," I said, because I believed that it was true.

"Well, that's good," he said. "It's a *fait accompli*, as the French would say."

He took a quick sip from his coffee, then stared at the steaming liquid as if something was not entirely to his liking. "Why don't you tell her how good life is up here in the wilderness?" he said. "Maybe that will entice her to come back and join the fun. Tell her your father is still managing to provide for you in the manner to which you've become accustomed."

Out on the water the heron's head shot forward. So fast I didn't even see it happen. One moment he was standing still and the next he was holding a struggling bluegill in his beak.

I set the last dish onto the counter. "All right," I said. "I can tell her those things."

After we finished the dishes we went outside to practice golf. This was a routine my father had insisted on since we'd come to live on the lake. He'd started playing the year before on a dusty par-three course in Grand Rapids, and he was anxious to master the fine points of the game and demonstrate his competence. Golf, he told me more than once, was an integral part of the selling formula. On a golf course you got to know a man in ways that were impossible in a business setting, and you could demonstrate your judgment and not be threatening or offensive.

Now, in the fading October sunlight, he bent over the ball, his hands wrapped lightly on the club shaft. As he prepared to take his shot he talked out loud, giving a summary of the thoughts he used to guide his stroke: the position of his feet, the angle of the clubface, the speed of the takeaway. All of this talk, I assumed, was for my benefit, a continuation of the never-ending learning process in which he put such store.

He made his shot. The ball arced beautifully through the twilight air and dropped within a couple of feet of a Hills Brothers coffee can.

"Now it's your turn, Danny." He straightened up, a smile on his face. "Just remember to hit through the ball. That's the secret of a good golf stroke."

I positioned myself over the ball. Golf to me was a game played by old men who had nothing better to do. I had no intention of demonstrating my judgment, or hitting through the ball, or following any of the other imperatives my father had mentioned. I took back the club in a long looping arc, then came down hard. The ball took off like a shot. But instead of heading for the coffee can it sailed over a row of cedar trees that bordered the yard.

"That was a worthy effort, son," my father said. "Nothing to be ashamed of. But now you get to learn the dark side of the game. How to recover from disaster."

Without a word I dropped the seven iron onto the grass and headed for the neighbor's yard, grateful to have a momentary reprieve from my father's lessons. Turning my back so I wouldn't get scratched, I pushed through the tangle of cedar branches. When I emerged on the other side I saw the neighbor girl standing near the back of her house. She was a tall skinny girl of about seventeen, and she wore red shoes and a white dress that the breeze whipped around her legs. I had seen her before, walking along the lakeshore or coming or going in a battered Chevrolet pickup truck. But I had never talked to her.

"Is this yours?" She held the golf ball in my direction.

"Yes," I said. I put out my hand for her to throw it to me.

"You need to be more careful," she said. She tossed the ball up into the air and caught it coming down. "I should probably throw it into the lake. That would teach you a lesson."

"Don't do that," I said. "It's worth thirty cents."

"There's people around that you could hurt, hitting wild like that."

"I don't see any people."

"There's me, for one. You could have hit me."

I took a couple of steps in the girl's direction. She had dark hair chopped off straight at her shoulders and a thin nose that looked too long for the rest of her face. The breeze from the lake folded the white dress against her body.

"You're the people who are renting the Michelson's place," she said. She threw the ball up into the air again, following it with her eyes. "But you don't look like what I expected."

"What did you expect?"

"I don't know. Some Italians from Detroit. Or hillbillies with a herd of goats. Maybe Cyclops with one eye."

Just then I heard a noise behind me. When I turned around I saw a group of sailboats headed toward a red buoy floating about a hundred feet offshore. The boats were heeled far over in the breeze. They seemed to struggle to make headway toward the buoy.

"That's the Wednesday night sailboat races," the girl said. "The rich people come out from town and use our lake for a little while. Then they go home and give it back to us."

"They don't look rich to me," I said. Out on the water, men were shouting back and forth and sails were flapping.

"Well maybe you know more about it than I do," the girl said. "Maybe you're rich, too."

"Not hardly," I said. "My dad sells things to hardware stores."

The girl tilted her head and looked at me in a funny way. "There's not too many hardware stores around here," she said. "Only cottages and run-down farms. Who's he going to sell to?"

"He travels," I said. "He travels around by car."

"Well, maybe he can do it then," the girl said, although she still sounded doubtful. "Traveling around."

We stood for a moment without saying anything. From the other side of the cedar hedge I heard my father call out: "It's getting too dark to see the ball, Danny. You better come inside."

I heard the door of our cabin open and close, then a

light came on in one of the windows and I saw my father's shape pass in front of it.

I turned back to the girl. "How come you're living out here on the lake?" I asked. "After Labor Day."

"This is where we live all the time. My parents and me." She turned and looked back at her house, a small tarpaper-sided structure that seemed more like a hunting shack than a place for a family to live in. "My father takes care of people's houses. Like fixing the roof when it leaks. He does taxidermy, too, when he can get it."

"So are you going to give me the golf ball?" I asked.

"I'm still thinking about it," the girl said. She threw the ball up into the air again, high this time, drifting to one side to make the catch. Then she started walking in my direction, taking slow graceful steps like she was in no particular hurry. Seeing her like that, with the breeze blowing out her dark hair and pushing the dress tight up against her body, I decided that she was pretty, and that other people would think so, too.

"Why you're only young," the girl said when she got close. "You looked older from back there."

"I'm sixteen," I said.

"Sure you are," she said. "And I'm twenty-five." She grinned a crooked smile.

"Anyway, I guess there's nothing wrong with that," she said. "Nothing that time won't cure." She held out her hand with the golf ball. "And I didn't mean what I said about throwing your golf ball in the lake. That was a comment meant for an older boy."

I reached out and took the golf ball from her hand.

"Now you'll have to do *me* a favor some day," she said.

"Okay," I said, although I couldn't imagine what I could do that would interest her.

She tilted her head back and looked at me through slightly narrowed eyes. "I don't suppose you know anything about geometry?" she said.

"Some," I said.

"I thought so. You've got that brainy look to you."

"I'm pretty good at math," I said, which was true.

"Well I'm an idiot in that particular category," the girl said. "That's why I'm taking geometry for the second time."

"Why don't you get help from your teacher?"

"I don't go to school this year," she said. She was so close I could see little flecks of lipstick on her mouth. "I take my classes at home."

She paused, still looking into my face, as if her statement had a special meaning that I should understand. It didn't, though, so I just stood there waiting for her to continue.

"They think I'll corrupt the other kids," she said, with another crooked smile. Then she pressed her hands against the front of her dress and smoothed the fabric over her stomach "I'm in the family way," she said, looking down at the tiny bulge that the tight fabric revealed. She tossed her head to get a strand of hair out of her face. "That's a high-class way of saying you're pregnant, in case you don't know about such awful things."

"I know what it means," I said. And I did, because my father had explained those things to me last year during a Sunday afternoon walk through Garfield Park. He had told me about love and explained how men and women copulate and how it was a thing that people did but not something you talked about. And then he explained how a girl kept from getting pregnant by keeping track of her cycles. And then he said that when I was older I should be careful not to get a girl in trouble, but that if I did it would be my fault and I should not expect help from him or anyone else.

"Does it shock you?" the girl asked. "My shameful condition."

"No," I said. "It's all right." And it *did* seem all right, because she was so relaxed about telling it to me, although it felt strange to have a pregnant girl standing so close and to hear her speak so calmly about a thing I knew to be a terrible sin. For a moment I tried to make it seem less strange by picturing her in bed with a boy, both of them in love and grabbing and holding each other under a blanket. But it was a hard thing to imagine and so I stopped.

During all the time that I was thinking, the girl remained silent, just standing and staring at me with no particular expression, as if it were my turn to say something important and she was waiting to hear what it would be. But I didn't know what to say, and so I just repeated, "It's all right" again, and then turned and looked out onto the lake.

It was almost dark now and hard to see much of anything. But then I spotted the sailboats on the far side of the lake, a cluster of dim gray triangles rocking slowly over a great flatness, heading in the direction of a larger boat bedecked with colorful flags. Then a puff of white smoke appeared like magic in the air above the larger boat, followed by the crack of a pistol shot reaching us across the water.

"That's the end of the race," the girl said, looking out. "Now they know who the winner is." She turned back to me. "Well, anyway, what you did say—little that it was—was very sweet. Too bad my boyfriend didn't feel the same way. He joined the Army when he heard about my delicate condition. He didn't even bother telling me."

"That's too bad," I said.

The girl looked at me sharply, as if I'd said something stupid. But then her expression changed and she smiled at me in a way that made her look tired. "I cried at first," she said. "I cried quite a lot. But now I'm reconciled to it. You can reconcile yourself to almost anything, you know. The main thing is that I love my baby and will take good care of it." She looked down at her stomach again and I knew that she was thinking about the baby growing there and how she would take good care of it. "Whether or not I've got a husband isn't important," she added. "Just as long as I'm a good momma."

I still didn't know what to say, although it seemed like a terrible thing that her boyfriend had done to her, and I wished I knew words that would make her feel better.

"What about *your* momma?" the girl said, looking up. She tossed her head again to get the strand of hair off her face. "I haven't seen any woman around your place."

I thought about how I should answer. All her talk about

getting pregnant and losing her boyfriend and having to take her classes at home had made me feel sorry for her, and I wanted to say something that would make her feel better about her life. And then I thought about my *own* mother at her parents' house in Boca Raton, and I wondered what she was doing that very minute, whether she was out in the back yard talking to a stranger about her life, or whether she was reading one of her poetry books, or whether she was getting ready to call me to tell me that she loved me. All of these thoughts ran together in my head so that I didn't have a single thought to say to the girl, but only a lot of half-thoughts that added up to nothing.

"My mother's dead," I said. "She died in an automobile accident."

A shocked expression came onto the girl's face. "Why that's terrible," she said. "You must feel awful."

"I did at first," I said. "But you get used to it. It's like what you said about your boyfriend."

Just then a screen door opened at the back of the tarpaper-sided house and a large woman stepped out onto the wooden stoop. The woman had on blue jeans and a red plaid shirt. She peered across the yard to where the girl and I were standing in the twilight.

"Amber, you better get in here," the woman said in a loud voice.

"I'm talking to our new neighbor, Momma. I'll be in in a minute."

"You better come in right now."

"Oh, Momma," she said. "He's only a boy."

"You heard me," the woman said.

The girl—Amber—turned to me. She put her hand on my arm and leaned in close. "I've got to go," she said in a kind of whispery voice. "Momma's been crazy since I got myself pregnant. She thinks all you boys have got just one thing on your mind."

I looked at Amber, surprised that she would think about me in that way. She had started to turn away, but she stopped with her hand still resting on my arm. "I'll tell you something," she said, and she leaned in so close that I could feel her hard stomach press against my arm. "If you ever get lonely for your own momma you can come over and talk to me." I felt her hard stomach and I felt the ends of her hair whipping my face in the breeze. "I'm a momma, too," she said. "So it'll be nearly the same thing." She smiled and squeezed my arm. Then she turned and walked back in the direction of her house, walking in that graceful way she had.

When I returned to the cabin my father was sitting in an upholstered chair next to the kerosene stove. Arranged around him on the floor were the things he called his peddler's gear—boxes of steak knives and key chains and ballpoint pens that he gave to people he wanted to sell things to. He was organizing them for the next day of selling.

I sat down at the kitchen table, and I got out my books and started to work on the Gettysburg Address. But I found it hard to concentrate and after a few minutes I pushed back and looked out the window, where everything was dark and gloomy. For a while I thought about my mother and I wondered when she would be calling. I'd told Amber that she was dead, which seemed like a terrible betrayal. And then I remembered a day last spring when my mother and I had driven up from Grand Rapids to Meridith to meet my father, who was going to show us the land where he planned to build our new house, and give us a glimpse of the brilliant new life that lay in store for us. We met him in the parking lot of the motel where he'd been living since coming to assume his salesman's duties in March. It was a sunny day and he was sitting on a metal lawn chair reading a newspaper and smoking a cigarette. When he saw us drive up he smiled and folded the newspaper and came over to the car.

"There's a pretty sight," he said, looking at my mother.

"Hello, Jim," my mother said. "Are you taking a sun bath?"

I got out of the car to move into the back seat. As I was standing on the gravel parking lot my father came around and draped his arm around my shoulders. "Hello, Bub," he said. "Have you been taking good care of your mother?"

"He's been my guardian angel, Jim," my mother said, looking across the passenger's seat. And I believed that she was thinking about her headaches and how I'd stayed home from school to read poetry and make hot compresses. "I could go to the moon and back and be safe with him," she added.

My father got into the passenger seat. Then he leaned over and kissed my mother on the mouth, putting his arm around her shoulder and holding her tight for what seemed like a very long time.

"My goodness," my mother said. She laughed and made a fanning motion with her hand, as if she needed air. "That's a nice how-do-you-do." And then she looked back over her shoulder to where I was sitting in the back seat. "Now you know what love looks like, Danny," she said, and she smiled in a way that made her look pretty.

Outside the kitchen window the wind moved a tree branch against the side of the cabin. It made a rough scraping sound, as if some burrowing animal were trying to get inside.

I closed my book and got up from the kitchen table. I went and stood in the doorway to the living room. After a moment my father noticed me and looked up from where he was working with his peddler's gear.

"I have an answer to your question," I said. "The one about the Negro slaves."

My father blinked a few times, as if he couldn't remember what I was talking about. But then he set aside the steak knives and looked up at me and smiled.

"Well let's hear it, Bub," he said.

I didn't know exactly what I was going to say. Any more than I knew why I'd told Amber that my mother was dead when she wasn't. *That* was just a thing that had come out of my mouth without any thought behind it, just a feeling that had arisen in me and been released. Something I'd said to make Amber feel better and not a thing to worry or feel ashamed about.

"They were innocent bystanders," I said. I put my hand on the doorjamb, as if to steady myself against some impending movement. "Like people who see an accident but can't do anything about it."

My father stared at me with a slightly perplexed expression, as if I were a stranger who had walked in out of the night. Then his gaze drifted back to the box of steak knives with the half-completed note.

"You said it differently than I would have," he said. "But that's pretty much what I thought, too."

I turned away and went back into the kitchen and sat down at the table where I'd been working on the Gettysburg Address. Soon my mother would be calling and I would speak to her. She would tell me that she loved me, because she was afraid of leaving those words unsaid, afraid of what that lack might mean. But I knew that she would not be coming back, that she had already set her mind to that conclusion, and so even though she spoke the words she would not mean them—not completely—not in the way that Amber loved the baby that was growing inside of her, which involved some loss. Some giving up.

Outside, the wind moved the tree branch against the side of our cabin. And I thought about the sailboats out there in the darkness being steered back to their moorings. And for a moment I tried to imagine how it would feel to be out there with them, out there on the open water, jostled by the waves and with the spray coming over the side and everything dark and moving and never-settled. And I actually made myself dizzy, confused and off balance, as if I'd been cut off from something and was alone in a wild and unforgiving place. And then I had to close my eyes until my breathing steadied and my heart stopped pounding and I felt calm again and at peace. Settled and composed. Strong. Unafraid of what lay ahead.

Automatic

You could almost say it didn't matter. That was her final thought about the incident and then she put it out of her mind.

For one thing, she was so thin these days. Not that she had ever been that well endowed to begin with, because she'd always tended to the slim side, just a waif her father used to say in that mocking voice of his. And then there was the nervous energy of the last few months, the craziness leading up to the separation from Lloyd, her with no appetite and crying all the time and just wasting away to almost nothing. So letting him take his little liberty there in the back of the doughnut shop (afternoon and all the bakers gone), letting it go on for a while, him holding her and speaking in that soft comforting voice, giving her that deep look. Well, there wasn't anything to it. It was like holding hands or giving someone a pat on the shoulder.

"Don't forget Sacramento," he said afterwards, draining the last of his coffee. "I need your answer by Wednesday. That's when they change the fare from super-saver to regular."

"Sure," she said, her back to him, buttoning up. "I remember."

She stood at the window and watched as he crossed the shopping center parking lot, leapt over a water-filled pothole reflecting back the gray Midwestern sky, hoisted himself into the red pickup with the county seal emblazoned on the door (sheaves of wheat and a Conestoga wagon, a rising sun behind).

He backed the truck around and her hand came up in a friendly wave. But instantly she could tell he did not see her, was evidently lost in thought (him with his responsibilities), and so she let her hand fall back to her side.

The brake lights blinked. He pulled out into traffic.

She pushed a wayward strand of hair back off her face.

And then there was Lloyd, her so-called husband, who phoned her every day at three. It was always the same time: three o'clock. Right when the afternoon rush began. Everyone wanting a doughnut or a brownie. Like their life depended on it. Finally, she told him to try another time.

"Try two," she said, passing change back to a customer, the phone cradled against her shoulder. "Or three-thirty. Three-fifteen, even. But three's no good, Lloyd. I got my hands full then."

But three was the only time he had. Three was when the clients (what they called the inmates now) took their exercise in the gym and Lloyd had a few solitary moments in his tiny office. Three was when he felt the need to talk, hear her calming voice. It was as if the tension of working in such a hard-luck place built up to where he couldn't take it any more, and then he got to three and so he called her. Automatic.

He was a counselor at the state reformatory at the edge of town, meeting with the boys in his cramped office, talking about their troubles, trying to figure out what made them tick, how they could be helped.

That word—reformatory—was a holdover from the old days. Lloyd had explained it to her once, how it dated from when they did things differently, actually tried to turn the boys into something useful—welders, car mechanics, plumbers—instead of just holding onto them until they were twenty-one.

But nowadays the world was different; time marches on, etc. There'd been cutbacks, calls for fiscal responsibility, priorities ordered and re-ordered. Now Lloyd with his little counseling office was one of the last hedges left against the chaos of the boys' past lives. And he felt the strain of it—Lloyd did—the constant pressure of so many young lives hanging by a thread.

There were other changes, too, creating tensions of a different sort. Because the things that brought the boys in were more serious now and violent—armed robbery, assault, homicide even—the whole sad catalogue of urban hopelessness. Things you wouldn't believe, things you didn't even want to think about (but that you did—Lloyd did—poor, tender-hearted Lloyd).

"It's not the danger that bothers me so much," he said, trying for the umpteenth time to make her understand.

"What then?"

"It's the way it makes life seem. So bleak. Like what's the point?"

But part of it was the danger and she understood that. Because there were incidents. All those boys jammed in together, day and night, it was inevitable. Last month it was Ernie Bacus, struck with a fire extinguisher in the laundry, now home on medical leave for who knew how long. Watching soap operas and doing jigsaw puzzles. Killing time until the headaches went away.

"A fire extinguisher!" Lloyd said. "Jack Myers heard it while he was walking in the hall. Two little sounds. Something hard hitting against something soft. Then silence."

She took a drag of her cigarette, set it in the notch of the algebra book lying open on the pastry showcase, exhaled two roiling streams of smoke.

"I'm not even supposed to be talking to you, Lloyd. We're in the middle of a separation, if you'd care to remember."

"Okay," he said. "I understand, Lorraine. But sometimes it feels like everything is coming apart up here and your voice is the only solid thing I got left to hold onto."

After a pause, he added: "Don't think I don't appreciate it."

He had started coming in three weeks ago, this man, every afternoon for coffee and a pecan roll. Wearing khaki pants and a khaki shirt with pencils and little rulers sticking out of the breast pocket. Every day the same clothes and always the same table, the one near the cash register, so he could talk to her between customers. He told her he inspected buildings for the county, wires and pipes and cement. Things a normal person would never think about. Sort of like a policeman for buildings. That's how he explained it.

"I would have never guessed there's such a job as that," she said.

"There's a lot that goes on with buildings that the average person doesn't know about. You wouldn't believe the half of it."

"I'm studying algebra in a night class at the community college," she blurted out, the most impressive claim she could lay her hands on in a hurried moment. "I plan to be an x-ray technician. You start with algebra."

"You don't say," he said, sipping his coffee.

"I suppose you know about algebra," she said. "Equations and such."

❆   ❆   ❆

Lloyd didn't understand that she had her own problems to deal with, her own shaky hold on the world, the
residue of an alcoholic father, a would-be farmer trying to
carve out a life on eighty dusty acres in Kalkaska County.
A life of hard work greased with alcohol, but with his
fists thrown in from time to time. And when those got
tired there was his voice, another weapon, maybe worse.
She was plagued with memories (times when *she* could
use a friendly shoulder to cry on): the old man standing outside her bedroom screaming curses about some
imagined offense, backlit by the hall light, his oversized
shadow sweeping the room, touching the bed, the walls,
the bureau, the bed again, like a toxic stain trying to gain a
foothold in her little girl's universe.

She'd come though it, sure, but not unscathed. She'd
learned that life is hard and that you couldn't count on
much. Most of all, she'd learned to stand on her own two
feet and to expect other people to do the same. She had
no tolerance for weakness, Lloyd's included.

"I'm not your shrink," she told him now, angry at another mis-timed phone call. "I can't help it that you're
afraid to be around criminals all day."

"They're not criminals," he said. "Not yet, anyway.
That's what I'm supposed to keep from happening. Anyway, it's got nothing to do with being afraid, Lorraine. I
told you, that's not what this is all about."

She paused, sorry now for what she'd said, trying to

think of something positive to end on, finish the conversation on a high note. Then she recalled the African violets that had struggled in the meager light of their bedroom window, those vivid blues and whites and greens.

"By the way, Lloyd, do you still have your violets? Those pretty violets that you raised."

"There's no room for them in my new apartment."

"That's a shame. You were so good with them. You should try to get some."

He was coming in regularly now, boasting about the buildings he inspected, the citations he wrote, how he made the contractors toe the line. She liked his swaggering manner, so full of himself, so different from Lloyd. And then one day he announced he was flying out to Sacramento to take a test. He wanted to inspect buildings out there, become qualified for that in California, where they had better weather. He would fly out on Thursday, come back Sunday, and he wanted her to come along. His treat. They'd spend the weekend in Sacramento having fun. Whatever it was people did in Sacramento for fun. They'd figure it out when they got there.

She raised her eyebrows, smiled. "I'm not entirely a free woman," she told him. "Things are sort of in midstream with me and Lloyd. Marriage-wise, I mean."

"Oh, well," he said, "you and him are living apart, right? That's the main thing."

"I guess," she said.

"The divorce is just follow-through. Slam dunk."

He stood up, balled his coffee cup and tossed it in the trash can, came around behind the counter and kissed her on the mouth, like it was expected.

"I consider myself a lady," she said. "Just in case you might like to know."

"Nobody's saying you're not," he said, grinning.

She gave Lloyd the news on Monday. Tried to do it gently, leave him with something he could take away. Give him that much, anyway.

"You're just too tender-hearted," was how she put it, sitting at the kitchen table. "And that's no good for me, Lloyd. You got to start looking out for yourself. Toughen yourself up some."

He cleared this throat. "You mean become a man."

"Oh, well, that word means different things," she said distractedly, thinking suddenly about her father.

Then, casting her own gaze sideways: "Anyway, I'm not the one to do it, Lloyd. It's not my job to prop you up. I got my own demons to wrestle with, in case you haven't noticed. In this world, everyone's on their own."

She felt his eyes lock on her face but kept her gaze nailed hard against the wall, pulled a quantity of air into her lungs, held it for a moment. "Anyway, I got a lawyer who can help us to end it. No big thing, Lloyd. Just a mistake that needs correcting." She tried to speak in an offhand voice, like commenting on yesterday's weather. "He said he can see us next Thurday at ten."

Wednesday and he came in all smiles, khaki shirt crisp, hair slicked back.

"What's the decision?" he asked.

"I'm still thinking," she said, in a playful tone of voice. Then, in mock confusion: "Where was it you wanted to take me? Sacramento, was it?"

He scowled, uncertain if she was kidding, not liking it if she was. And then the phone rang.

It was Lloyd, of course, his voice with that funny edge, no doubt wanting his daily dose of whatever it was he took from her.

"I've been thinking about something, Lorraine," he said excitedly.

"I have to call you back, Lloyd," she said, cupping the mouthpiece with her hand.

"You know how this place is making me crazy?" he continued

"It's just like I been telling you, Lloyd. Only we got to talk about it later."

Across the counter she saw him check his watch, regard her in a questioning way, eyebrows raised.

"I've been thinking about something, Lorraine. Just hear me out now. Do you suppose I could get a job in landscaping? I've been thinking about that all morning. About plants and flowers."

"I suppose," she said, "but I can't talk now, Lloyd." Her free hand rose, settled at her throat.

"Growing things has always been a particular love of mine. You know that."

She turned so that her back was to the counter, rubbed her forehead with two stiff fingers. "I imagine you'd be good at it, Lloyd. I can picture you with flowers. Sure."

Just then she sensed a movement, felt a hand close over hers where it gripped the phone. She turned to face him, covering up the mouthpiece, gave a quick stiff smile. "I've got a little situation here," she whispered. "It'll only take a minute."

He leaned in close, his belly flattened against the counter's edge. "I want an answer,'" he said fiercely. "Is it Sacramento or not? That's not such a hard choice, is it?"

She met his stare, felt his fingers covering hers, heard Lloyd's voice buzzing on the wires. "What do you say, Lorraine? Should I give landscaping a try?"

A nervous smile passed over her face. She tried to step back and open up some space between them, but he tightened his grip and smiled at her in a taunting way, as if it was a game they were engaged in now, her the captive owing him an answer. On her side, though, it was no game: she felt the stirring of a memory, a shadow passing over, a jolt of panic.

She pulled back hard and broke his grip, lost her balance and stumbled back against the donut case, setting the glass doors rattling in their metal tracks like vibrating plates of steel. "Don't touch me," she snarled. "Don't you dare touch me."

"God almighty," he said. "I'm dealing with a crazy woman."

She crouched behind the counter like a cornered animal. Then she stood, smoothed her dress, tried to swallow the choking feeling in her throat.

"You almost made me break the glass," she said, giving a nervous laugh.

She rubbed her shoulder where it'd smacked against the donut case, then looked again in his direction, but his angry stare forced her eyes away. And then she spotted the phone dangling crazily from its spiral cord, like a dancing puppet on a string, and suddenly she remembered Lloyd out there at the reformatory, him with his quiet ways and serious demeanor, his tendency to stretch himself for the sake of those poor boys until he almost broke apart himself. Still waiting for her answer.

She reached down and grabbed the phone.

"It's me back," she said, breathing hard, working to keep her voice level. "I dropped the phone." Then: "What was that you were saying, Lloyd? About the flowers and plants? It's something to consider, I suppose. But you don't want to act too quick. You're awfully good at what you're doing now. Helping boys and such."

Across the counter she saw him smile, shrug, then turn and start to walk away.

"Why'n't you come over to the house tonight, Lloyd?"

she said, watching his back as he passed out through the door. "Maybe we can figure things out over dinner."

She bagged up the remainders and put them into the day-old bin. Then she slid the bank deposit bag into the special nighttime hiding place next to the refrigerator. She switched off the lights, stepped out through the front door, closed and locked it behind her.

The parking lot was empty, the only light a street lamp humming overhead. An evening breeze cooled her face and arms, ruffled the surface of a puddle, moved an empty cigarette carton across the expanse of endless asphalt.

For a moment she stood beneath the mercury vapor beam, captured in its brilliance, thinking about what had happened that afternoon, the chance she'd thrown away. Probably just a wild weekend in Sacramento; but maybe something more: a whole new life of comfort and security, who could know for sure? Anyway, she'd made her choice, was going back to Lloyd now. That was a fact she had to live with, and maybe not so bad a one at that.

She stepped out of the circle of light and headed for the far end of the parking lot, where her car was, her solitary footsteps echoing in the hollow spaces between the buildings. She clutched her handbag tighter. And then, to fortify her spirits, she thought of Lloyd, imagined him as he was that very moment, seated in his cramped office at the reformatory, a man surrounded by all manner of life's problems, like a soldier manning a lonely outpost.

She reached her car and started to unlock it. And then she heard a noise, a little scuffing sound, coming from just behind her. She whirled, one arm upraised, looked frantically right and left, tried to spot the danger that was always lurking in the shadows. But all she saw was the cigarette carton being pushed across the asphalt by the fitful wind, making little scraping sounds with each lurch forward.

Marseille

I was stretched out on the living room sofa and Loretta was in the kitchen talking on the phone to her best friend Joan. I had just made a run to the 7-Eleven to get some cigarettes, and I was smoking them now while Loretta said whatever she had to say to Joan.

I would have to admit that I was in an odd frame of mind. That afternoon I'd lost my job at the injection molding factory in Saginaw. Just before the first shift ended Sammy Niswick called me in and said that orders were way down. It was the state of the economy, he said, the goddamned economy. So they had to cut payroll. It was unfortunate but they had no choice. He knew I'd understand.

So now I was unemployed. Out of work. Without a livelihood. But I hadn't told Loretta yet because I didn't want
her to worry. I was thinking that maybe I could line up a
new job before I had to tell her about the one that I had
lost. That way the lost job would seem to be of little con-
sequence. Or part of a larger plan I'd had in mind all along.

Over on the other side of the living room, Ben was
leading our black lab Charlie around by the collar. He
was talking to the dog in a voice you'd use with a misbe-
having child.

"You come here," Ben said. "You bad dog, Charlie, you
come here." He pulled Charlie's collar and Charlie took a
few shifty steps forward.

I raised my head up from the sofa. "Take it easy on poor
old Charlie," I said.

"I want him over in the corner," Ben said. "He's supposed to be a guard dog and that's where he belongs."

"Take it easy on him," I said. "Maybe he doesn't want
to guard today."

Ben ignored me. He hauled Charlie over to the corner
and pushed down on his haunches. When that didn't work
he leaned his whole little body over Charlie's rear end,
just hanging with his feet up off the floor. Charlie settled
himself, one inch at a time, then sat quietly where Ben had
put him, his large dark eyes staring straight ahead.

I lay my head back down on the sofa. All my life I'd
worked at one thing or another, but I'd never actually
had to *look* for a job. It seemed like whenever I *wanted*
a job there was always one waiting for me. But now that

I needed one I wasn't sure how to go about finding it. I thought there were probably special tricks you had to know about—how to present yourself to best advantage, for example, or cozy up to the people who were going to make the decision—and I should find out what they were. Then I wondered if it was possible that I would *not* find a job, that I would stay unemployed for months and months, or even forever, like the stories you hear about the Great Depression, or people in places like Mississippi or the old mill towns of New England—and what *that* would do to a man, whether it would make you feel worthless and cheap, or if you could learn to like it.

Out in the kitchen I heard Loretta hang up the telephone. I knew I should go in and talk to her. If I wasn't going to tell her about losing my job I needed to talk to her about *something*. Otherwise she'd get suspicious.

I pushed up from the sofa and headed into the kitchen. Loretta was standing by the window looking out at the back yard where the summer sun was still bright. She had a pleasant smile on her face.

"I told Joan we'd meet her and Mel later at the Empire Cafe for coffee and cheesecake," she said, turning around. "I'm going crazy from being in this house all day." She made a face and rolled her eyes like she was going crazy. "I'll get a sitter for Ben and Stacie."

I changed my mind about talking to Loretta. I guess I couldn't bear to spoil the pleasant mood she was in. And I realized something else too: I had to think some more about what my next step was going to be.

"Okay," I said.

I turned and headed for the basement.

In the basement I've got an old wing chair next to the furnace and a gooseneck lamp for when I want to read. From my chair I can see my fishing gear stored on metal shelves along the wall: tackle boxes, Shakespeare rods and reels, boxes of Mustard hooks, spools of monofilament line. Stuff I haven't had time to use in years. Over on the other wall my tools hang in neat rows on the pegboard: screwdrivers, pliers, crescent wrenches, saws. A place for everything and everything in its place.

To get my mind off my troubles I thought about a conversation I'd had a few days ago with this young woman at work, Sophie Barrieux, who programs computers in Accounting. Sophie is from Marseille in France and went to college there. Don't ask me how she ended up in Saginaw; I guess such things are not unexpected in this global world we live in. Our conversation was nothing special but for some reason it'd stuck in my mind. Sophie told me about her family back in Marseille, two brothers and a sister, plus her parents and grandparents, all of whom lived together in a single house. There were cousins and aunts and uncles, too, and she described each one in detail and said how much she loved them. She told me about her father, who went out every day in a small boat to fish for cod and haddock, and about the house that she'd grown up in, which wasn't like houses here but just a narrow building on a city street. She told me about the school where she had been taught by nuns, and about the market where her mother went each day to get their fruits and vegetables.

Then my thoughts swung away from Sophie and I thought about *my* life and how it was turning out differently from what I'd expected a few years ago. I was only thirty-two but already responsibilities were piling up on me. I had two kids who needed food and clothes and toys. I had a mortgaged house where things kept breaking down. I had a dog who liked to chew the furniture. I had little Stacie and all her asthma medicines.

I had no time to fish and hunt and do the other things I used to do.

And now I didn't have a job.

After a while I came up from the basement carrying my fly rod and my rubber waders. I was feeling a little better because I'd made a few decisions. I realized that being unemployed opened up some possibilities.

I went over and set the waders on the kitchen counter. They humped on the yellow Formica like something that belonged someplace else. There was a little hole where the waders had rubbed against the furnace and I was going to fix it.

Loretta was standing over by the kitchen sink with a

glass of milk in her hand. I felt her watching as I went to work on the waders. I got the patch kit out with the tube of glue. I squeezed some glue out and started to spread it with that little stick they give you. After a minute Loretta said, "What's up, Tom?"

I kept spreading out the glue. When I pulled the stick away a trembling thread stretched back. It held for a second, then snapped.

"I thought I'd drive out to the river and do some fishing before it gets dark," I said. "Like I used to do before we got married."

I pressed the rubber patch over where I'd spread out the glue. The glue squeezed out and made a little hump around the edges.

"That sounds like fun," Loretta said. "Maybe I'll come too. I can have the sitter come early. Then we can go meet Joan and Mel at the Empire Cafe."

My patch looked good so I put the waders on the floor and began to check the plastic box that held my flies. They were all mixed up in the different little chambers: McGinties, Blue Dunns, nymphs. Plus a lot I couldn't remember the names of.

"You don't fish, Loretta," I said. "You're no good at it."

"I know," she said. "But I can sit on the bank and read. I'm good at that. I'll take a folding chair."

I dumped the flies out on the counter. They were all tangled up. Some of the feathers had come loose.

Loretta turned around and raised herself on tiptoes so she could look out the little window over the kitchen sink.

"It's nice out," she said. "The sunset will be gorgeous on the river."

I stopped working with my flies and went over to the window and looked out. I saw a rusty swing set, an empty clothesline with plastic clips, a dog run with bare earth showing, a charcoal grill full of rainwater.

I turned and looked at Loretta. "I thought I might start to do some of the things I liked to do before. Like fishing."

"You should, sweetheart," she said with a bright smile. "I vote yes to that."

I went back to sorting out my flies. "I thought maybe I'd just go out fishing by myself this time, Loretta."

Loretta got quiet. I sat arranging the flies.

"Look," I said, still looking down, "maybe I'd like to be alone for a while. Maybe I've got some things I'd like to think about. That's not asking too much, is it?"

I heard water running. Then I heard the milk glass get set down.

"What's the matter, Tom?" Loretta said.

"I'm all right. I've just been thinking about some things, that's all."

"What kind of things?"

At first I didn't answer. I knew if I answered I'd have to look at Loretta and then I'd probably say too much. But after a minute I couldn't take it any longer so I stopped and looked up anyway.

"I've been thinking I'd like to see some different places, Loretta," I said. That's one of the things I've been thinking about. Because there's a lot of places I haven't seen yet."

I thought Loretta would say something but she didn't. So I braced up and went ahead.

"And I'd like to go back to Cheboygan and see my folks again. Maybe go pheasant hunting with Dad. That's something I'd like to do too."

Loretta picked up a dishcloth, still looking at me.

"And I'd like to try a different job," I said, raising my voice a little. "I'm tired of standing in front of a molding machine all day. I'd like to do something that gets me out in the bounty of Mother Nature."

Loretta fingered the dishcloth but she didn't stop looking.

"And I'd like to get drunk," I said. "I'd like to get drunk once in a while and come home at three in the morning and sleep until noon. And I'd like to have friends who wanted to know my opinion about things. And I'd like to go to parties with people who laughed at what I said."

I was done talking then and Loretta could tell. She folded the dishcloth into a tiny square and put it down and turned and looked out the window. I went back to sorting out my flies.

"I told Joan we'd meet her and Mel at eight," she said. "But if you don't want to do it, Tom, that's all right. I don't care."

I thought for a minute about telling Loretta I didn't want to go to the Empire Cafe, but I decided that would be taking things too far. I knew I'd brought myself up to the edge of something, but I didn't know if I wanted to push over. Sometimes when you push over you can't come back.

"No" I said, after a quiet moment had passed. "It's okay. I'll meet you guys at the Empire Cafe. I'll meet you there at eight or eight-thirty."

Loretta went over and stood by the sink. She picked up the dishcloth that she'd just folded and started to polish the coffeepot. Then she said: "I'm going out to water the rhododendrons."

After another minute I picked up my plastic box of flies, all arranged in their neat little chambers. It was the first time they'd been arranged in years and that made me feel good.

Out along the river bank the sunlight sparkled on the water like little bursts of fireworks. At the curving far bank the current rippled along in moving patterns. Everything was lit up yellow from the setting sun: the overhanging trees, the rocks piled up along the river's edge, some water birds wading stiff-legged in the reeds.

I clumped down the bank in my rubber waders and splashed out into the water. The water rose up against my legs, the pressure folding the waders tight up against my thighs. I felt the odd dry-coolness of the river water on my legs, and I felt the little tugging pressure of the current. I braced up and shuffled forward on the gravelly bottom.

Later, after I'd finished fishing, I sat on the bank in the fading twilight, feeling good about the world and all it had to offer. Three trout were lined up at the water's edge, their opal skins seeming to hold the daylight. They lay on the muddy bank and seemed to glow.

I felt something in my fishing vest. When I reached in I found a silver flask with whisky, a remnant of some long-forgotten fishing trip. I uncapped the flask and took a good long swallow. Then I put it back.

A half-hour later I walked into the Empire Cafe still wearing my fishing vest. Being out on the river had felt good and I was anxious for that good feeling to continue. It seemed like the day had finally taken a positive turn. Even my lost job didn't bother me because I was beginning to see the opportunities it opened up for me.

At a table near the back I spotted Loretta and Joan and Mel. Joan has this bright red hair and Mel was wearing his checkered golf hat with the plastic No. 19 flag. They saw me coming and looked up.

"Here's the great white hunter," Mel said, smiling.

"Fisherman," I said. "The great fisherman."

"Whatever you say," Mel said. "Did you catch anything?"

"Three," I said. "I caught three."

"Hooray!" said Joan. "Loretta, you won't starve now. Tom has caught you some fish."

Loretta didn't smile or look up. She touched the handle of the coffee mug steaming in front of her.

"What kind of bait did you use?" Mel said.

"Not bait," I said. "Flies."

"Aren't flies bait?" said Joan.

"No," Loretta said, still staring at the mug. "Bait is like worms and grasshoppers. Flies are like little hooks with feathers."

"That's right," I said. I looked over and smiled at Loretta but she didn't look back.

"I know a few things," she said. She touched the handle of her mug.

I went up to the counter to get a coffee. When I came back Joan was giving Loretta a sly smile. I could tell they'd been talking about the conversation we'd had back at the house.

Mel leaned forward and rested his elbows on the table. "So when are you going to take me fishing, buddy?" he asked.

"It's not that easy, Mel," Joan said, jumping in before I could get an answer back to Mel. "Tom doesn't let just anyone come fishing with him. Ask Loretta."

"Ask Loretta what?" said Mel.

"Tom wouldn't let Loretta come out fishing with him tonight. He said he wanted to be alone."

"Don't get anything started, Joan," Loretta said. "It isn't worth it."

We all got quiet for a while. Mel caught my eye and smiled and raised his eyebrows. Then Joan said, "Loretta, I got those new drapes today. For the master bedroom. You should see them."

"Like the ones you were talking about?" said Loretta.

"They're sort of striped," said Joan. "Yellow and orange."

"More like maroon," Mel said. "Or maybe russet. I think I'd call it russet."

Joan drew back her head and stared wide-eyed at Mel, like she was amazed he would know such a word as russet. Then she looked at Loretta and laughed. "Anyway, you've got to see them, Loretta," she said.

"I'd like to," said Loretta.

I looked around the table. All the talk about drapes sounded crazy. I wanted to talk about something important. I wanted the conversation to be worthy of the good feelings that had got started out on the river.

"Why are we talking about drapes?" I said. "Can't we come up with something better than that?"

Joan and Loretta looked at me. Mel gave a little chuckle. Then he said: "Okay, here's something. I heard an interesting thing on the radio today. When I was driving in my car."

"Oh," said Joan.

"It's about farms," Mel said. "How they're all disappearing."

Joan looked at Mel. "That doesn't make any sense, honey. Where's our food going to come from?"

"That's not what I mean," Mel said. He raised one hand like he was trying to hold Joan back. "I mean there's less farmers. Less family farms. Less people farming."

"I see what he's getting at," said Loretta. "It's like the same amount of land is out there but there's fewer people working on it."

"That's right," Mel said. "Less farmers in the world. We're all factory workers now."

"My husband the brilliant sociologist," Joan said. She half-stood and leaned across the table. Mel half-stood and kissed her.

"It's true," Mel said.

Joan settled back and sipped her coffee. Then she said, "Tom and Loretta don't need farms anyway. Tom can fish for their food. They can live on trouts and bluegills."

I was starting to get angry at Joan and her big mouth. She kept wanting to bring the focus back on me. Plus the level of conversation still left something to be desired.

"Now we're stuck on farms." I said. "Can't we do better than that?"

"You're free to talk about anything you want," Joan said. She sat back and folded her arms and stared at me with that red hair. "Okay, everybody," she said. "Tom's got the floor."

They all turned and looked in my direction, Joan and Mel and Loretta. I tried to think of a subject worthy of the occasion: four good friends together and the whole world at our beck and call. But all I could think of was that conversation I'd had the other day with Sophie.

"Does anyone know anything about Marseille?" I asked.

Mel scrunched up his face. "Marseille?" he said. "That's on the Mediterranean, right?"

"That's right," I said.

"I saw a documentary about it once," he said. "Wait a minute. I'm thinking of Barcelona."

"Barcelona's Spain, Mel," Joan said. "Marseille's France."

"I know that," Mel said. "I just got mixed up for a minute."

"Why do you want to know about Marseille, anyway?" asked Loretta.

"I met someone from there," I said. "It sounded like a nice place. A beautiful city with people who like the life they live there."

"Why not ask *that* person about it?" said Joan. "Ask the person who lives there, not us."

I saw it'd been a mistake to bring up Marseille. Apparently, nobody was interested in talking about Marseille.

"Never mind," I said. "It's not important."

Joan sipped her coffee and made a face like she'd tasted something sour. Then she said, "Well, that was a vast improvement on the conversational scene." Mel laughed.

I thought I'd give the situation one more try; one final chance to take things to a higher plane. I reached into the pocket of my fishing vest where I had that silver flask. I uncapped it and poured some whisky into Loretta's coffee.

"What's that?" she said.

"I thought we could liven things up," I said, grinning. I poured some whisky into Joan's cup, too.

"Heh," Joan said. "That's my coffee. You went and ruined it."

"I made it better," I said. "We'll have a little party. Try it."

Joan looked at me across the table as if I was an alien who had dropped out of the sky. "I think Tom's going crazy on us, Loretta," she said.

"Just try your coffee, Joan," I said, getting angry. "I made it into Irish coffee. It'll be fun."

Suddenly everything got quiet. I sat with the silver flask in my outstretched hand. Mel gave a nervous laugh. Joan picked up a spoon and began to study it. Loretta stared off at the other side of the room.

That's when I decided I'd had enough. I looked around the Empire Cafe. Next to our table there was a door with a metal handle. I stood up and pushed the metal handle and went out through the door. I found myself in a kitchen with bright lights and noise. Flames licked the blackened undersides of steaming pots. Waiters called orders back and forth through a little window.

I walked across the kitchen and went out through a second door. I didn't know where I was going. All I knew is that I had to get away.

I was standing at the end of a dark alleyway. Plastic garbage bags lay scattered on the ground. A gray cat crouched beneath a dumpster, its long tail twitching around its meager body.

I started to smoke a cigarette, pulling in the smoke and blowing it out in narrow streams. At the far end of the alley I saw a street with lights and traffic and people passing on the sidewalk. It reminded me of a play, characters coming on stage and then moving off.

The cat watched me, its quiet eyes shining back little points of light.

I began to think about Marseille again. I pictured a harbor filled with fishing boats flying colorful sails, graceful parks with happy people strolling on gravel pathways, a market place with vendors selling cheeses and fresh vegetables, flowers and exotic pastries, and in the background big churches rising up against green hills with domes and crosses.

Just then I heard the door open behind me, followed by a rush of warm air. A hand reached out and touched my arm.

"Are you all right, Tom?" Loretta said.

"I'm fine, Loretta."

"Are you coming back inside?"

"I don't know. I sort of like it out here."

We were silent for several long minutes, Loretta with her hand resting on my arm, me watching the people passing on the street.

Finally I said, "There's something I want to tell you, Loretta."

"Oh," she said. She came around and stood in front, looked up into my face.

I tried to get my thoughts together but they were all mixed up. I wanted to finish the conversation I'd started inside the Empire Cafe—about Marseille—or tell Loretta how good it had felt to be out on the river. But Loretta has got this special way of looking at you; she has these quiet eyes that can gather you up.

I took a deep breath and held it. I let my mind go blank. Then I said the first thing that came back into it.

"I've got to find another job, Loretta," I said.

"Oh," she said, still looking at me with those quiet eyes.

"Yes," I said. "I was fired today. Me and a lot of other guys."

Loretta stared up into my face for what seemed like a long time. Then her gaze moved off and she looked over my shoulder, narrowing her eyes like she was focusing on something far, far away. I didn't dare say another word until I knew what she was thinking. I was afraid she was going to start to cry, or get mad and tell me I was a failure, or go back inside the Empire Cafe where Joan and Mel were waiting. But finally her gaze came back. "That Joan," she said. She smiled in a sad way and shook her head like she was filled with deep regret. "Sometimes I think she should just mind her own damn business."

And that's when I bent down and kissed Loretta. Because I knew she was on my side again. And Loretta, she stood up on her tiptoes and kissed me back, touched my neck with her smooth cool hand, pulled up tight against me. And it was nice to be kissing her like that, nice to know I wasn't alone now. But I've got to tell you it felt odd, too, because those thoughts of Marseille were still inside my head. I guess I would have to say that it felt odd but normal. Like Loretta and Marseille had joined together into a single splendid thought.

After a while we finished kissing, but I kept my arms around Loretta, holding tight against her, taking care to keep my cigarette away so I wouldn't burn her. Over her shoulder people kept passing on the street.

Hesitation

Just before Norman Miles left his house to report for the night shift at the municipal transit company, where he drove a city bus, he had an argument with his wife, Carol. It was about the way he'd acted with this blond woman in the Firefly Lounge on Saturday night. To Norm's way of thinking his behavior had been completely innocent, just some idle conversation with a stranger standing next to him in a crowded bar, and that was how he explained it now to Carol. And maybe if that was all it had been, conversation, Carol would have been okay. But at one point during the evening Norm had carried things a little further than conversation. For reasons that were still unclear to him he'd told the woman—this pretty woman who was a perfect stranger—a slightly crude joke, one he'd heard from Larry Tork last Thursday in the locker room at the transit company, a joke that had to do with breasts.

Norm, standing now in the kitchen of his small tract house, about to leave for work, could not explain to Carol why he had told the joke to the woman, and he understood that the absence of a reason weakened his defense. If forced to guess, he would have said it had something to do with the odd feeling that had overtaken him since achieving the status of a twenty-year man at the municipal transit company—a milestone celebrated only last week with a small ceremony presided over by the night-shift manager and involving the presentation of a silver pin, and some cake. In any case, whatever the reason, Norm had done it, had told the slightly-crude joke to the strange pretty woman he'd met at the bar, all while gazing fixedly into her eyes, though still possessing enough composure to remember to raise his voice so that Carol, who was standing behind him, would hear the joke, too, and be included in the fun.

And probably even *that* would have been okay with Carol—having to peer over Norm's shoulder as he told a slightly crude joke to a strange pretty woman in a bar—except that when Norm got to the end, to the punch line, he'd spread his hands and held them out in front, just inches from the pretty woman's chest. It was a deliberate, although unplanned, gesture, a way to add a bit of showmanship to the punch line, Norm supposed;

harmless, really, in its own peculiar way, admittedly slightly shocking, but nevertheless an innocent gesture done for fun on a Saturday night in the Firefly Lounge.

But Carol hadn't seen it that way. She had not seen it that way at all. What she had seen was the crudeness of Norm's gesture, the fact that the woman was pretty, and the fact that the woman, at the joke's conclusion, had seemed to smile at Norm and toss her hair, as if daring him to do what the gesture implied.

Norm saw this, too, saw the pretty woman's expression, kind of a challenge, possibly, or maybe merely surprise, but in any case enough of an encouragement to cause Norm, who had once aspired to be a hunting guide in northern Michigan, to hold his hands there—just inches from the strange woman's breasts—longer than he needed to, longer than was necessary for the joke to work, certainly, and longer than he would have done if he had been thinking straight in the first place. But to Carol, who was okay with it being only a crude joke, Norm's hesitation gave the situation an altogether darker meaning. Norm's hesitation made Carol understand that the joke wasn't the issue and had not been from the start. What the issue was, Carol understood now, was not the joke, or the pretty woman, or even the pretty woman's breasts, but Norm himself, or at least that part of him that after twenty-three years was still a mystery to her; the part that spent long hours in his basement workshop doing God-knows-what, that part that could be glum and surly for no good reason, and that preferred to work the night shift at the transit company, even though he'd long ago qualified for days. In short, it was that secret part of Norm that—for all Carol knew—might actually consider doing what the shocking gesture implied.

And Norm *had* considered doing it. He admitted this to Carol, considered placing his hands on the pretty woman's breasts, not in a rough, ungentlemanly way, but only lightly, as a gesture, an appropriate gesture, actually, that would further enhance the punch line of his joke. But beyond the obvious considerations—what the consequences might be, good or bad—Norm had also wondered this: how it would be as an experience, possibly a once-in-a-lifetime experience for a man who drove a city bus but had wanted to be a hunting guide in northern Michigan, holding a strange woman's breasts in the middle of a crowded bar, and for no other reason than to enhance the punch line of a joke.

And so Norm had hesitated, his hands suspended in an awkward, conspicuous way, the crowd around the bar grown quiet, customers craning their necks and jostling for position, his wife Carol peering over his shoulder, the pretty woman fixing him with her surprised or possibly challenging gaze, and Norm, the center of these forces, believing he had arrived at a certain point in his life, a point where he could show himself to be the man he truly was, or could be: someone who defied convention, broke the social contract, acted like a hunting guide in northern Michigan, and with impunity.

But—as fast and unexpected as the moment had come, it was past. The time to act, if it had existed at all (and Norm, whenever he thought about it later, was sure that it had), was gone, punctuated by a long, low whistle from someone in the back of the crowd, followed by a ripple of dismissive laughter, followed by the strange pretty woman grinning and turning away, resuming a conversation with her girl friend standing on her other side.

And Norm, staring at thin air—or, more precisely, at the back of the pretty woman's blond head—dropped his hands from the fruitless, hovering position where the woman's breasts had been (or nearly been) an instant ago, and turned back to his wife, Carol, on his other side, who was regarding him with much the same shocked expression she wore now, in the kitchen of their small tract house, as Norm, clasping his battered lunchbox in one hand and a dog-eared copy of *Field and Stream* in the other, prepared to leave for the night shift at the transit company, where for eight long hours he would navigate a city bus through darkened streets, avoiding, by skill and quiet courage, the untold perils lurking in the urban landscape, a job that he performed with splendid ease, and knew himself to be the master of.

Scout

The old church sat in a dreary, run-down section of the city. It could be seen from far away, its massive square shape thrusting up above the small houses that surrounded it. The main building containing the sanctuary was plain and solid looking, built as though it would last forever, with brick walls that the years had transformed into a mottled brown. Perfectly centered along the front was a thin tapering spire. Although rising high above the roof it did little to alter the building's earthbound appearance. In spite of its divine purpose, the old structure seemed rooted in the soil, perhaps reflecting, in brick and mortar, the sturdiness and muted aspirations of its Midwestern parishioners.

In just a few more years nothing about the church would

matter any more. It and the surrounding houses would be torn down to clear a path for a new expressway, a civic project that would improve the flow of traffic through the city and win for the city fathers a commendation for forward-thinking government from a national magazine. But now, in 1956, the bleak edifice stood and endured, just as it had stood and endured for more than a hundred years.

Sam and Jimmy walked along Bridge Street on their way to a Boy Scout meeting in the basement of the church. It was a Saturday afternoon in March. The air was filled with a sullen dampness left over from a rainstorm the night before. The sky was the color of concrete.

Sam walked in front. He was a tall, thin boy with sandy-blond hair and he moved with long easy strides. The other boy had dark hair and a lazy, ambling sort of walk.

"For crying out loud, hurry up," Sam said.

"We've got plenty of time," Jimmy said. "In fact, we're probably going to be early."

"I don't care," Sam said. "I'd rather get there early, even if we have to wait around."

"That's an interesting concept," said Jimmy.

Sam turned around and started to say something back to Jimmy but he caught himself and stopped. He hated it when Jimmy said things that didn't make sense. Lately, everything for Jimmy was a "concept." It was as if that was the only word he knew.

"By the way," Jimmy said from behind, "my Mom told me you're supposed to come back to our house after the meeting."

"Oh," said Sam.

"Your Mom's going to pick you up on her way back from the hospital."

Sam slowed down. A tiny buzz began to churn away in his chest. It was like a little animal was trapped inside and trying to get out. It was a feeling Sam had gotten used to during the last few days.

"Did she say anything else?"

"Not that I know of."

Sam pictured his father lying in a hospital bed with his mother seated next to him.

"How's your Dad doing now?" said Jimmy.

With an effort Sam pushed the image out of his head. The buzzing feeling began to go away. Then Sam took a deep breath and it went away completely, like a candle being snuffed out. "He's fine," he said to his friend.

"When's he coming home?"

"Huh?" said Sam.

"When's your Dad coming home?"

"The doctors say it'll be a while yet. I guess they don't know for sure."

"Have they let you see him?"

"Sure. Only you can't have a regular conversation. He's in an oxygen tent."

"An oxygen tent," Jimmy said. "What's that?"

Sam slowed down to let his friend catch up. "It's like a plastic sheet they hang over the bed and pump full of oxygen." Sam spread his arms to suggest the dimensions. "It makes it easier for sick people to breathe. But it's hard to have a conversation. It's like trying to talk through a curtain."

"That's very interesting."

Sam looked quickly at his friend. "What's so interesting about it?"

"Well, nothing, I guess."

"But you said it was interesting. That an oxygen tent is interesting. I don't see it myself, so I'm asking you."

"Just forget it. I didn't mean anything."

They passed a small park where a young woman sat on a green slatted bench with a baby carriage next to her. Jimmy watched the woman roll the carriage back and forth and make little sounds to the child. As the boys passed the woman looked up and smiled at them.

"Are you going to stay in Scouts next year?" Sam asked.

"I don't think so," the shorter boy said. "I'm tired of all the marching around and wearing badges. It's childish."

Sam considered this for a moment. "But some of the stuff is pretty fun. The campouts."

"Yeah, but I can go camping by myself if I want to."

"And there's the stuff that you learn. My Dad said the Boy Scouts teach you things for later in life. Like how to act right and do things with your hands. He said the Scout oath is about all that a person needs to know to get by in the world."

"Oh, yeah?" said Jimmy. He grinned. "That's an interesting concept."

Suddenly they arrived at the church. The flat brick walls seemed to appear all at once, towering over them. Sam ran up the front steps. He tried the brass doorknob on the arched wooden door but it didn't move. He shook the doorknob in frustration.

"I told you we were early," said Jimmy, coming up. He smiled at his friend. "So what do you suggest we do now?"

Sam walked down the steps and stood on the sidewalk. He looked up the street at the row of small wood-framed houses painted in browns and grays and greens. The only bright thing in sight was a blinking red traffic light two blocks away. Its slow, measured pulsing seemed to mirror something inside of Sam.

Sam turned and looked in the other direction where a narrow alley ran along the side of the church. He knew that it led to a small gravel parking lot in back. He had seen it once, a weed-choked plot of ground just large enough to hold two or three cars.

"Come on," Sam said. "Let's see if we can find another way in."

The two boys started down the alley, stepping around the mud puddles. Sam felt the air grow darker and colder as the high wall of the church cut off a section of the sky. When they reached the end of the alley Sam saw a woman lying against the brick wall of the church. At first it looked like a pile of rags had gotten caught in the weeds. But then Sam saw the nylon-stockinged legs and the shiny black shoes.

He stopped. The woman looked like she was asleep. Her hands were folded on her lap.

"Let's get out of here," Sam said.

Jimmy turned around and looked at his friend. "Come on" he said, grinning. "Haven't you seen a drunk before?"

Sam looked uncertainly at the woman. He took a few halting steps forward. Then the two boys moved forward together, side by side. When they got within a few feet Sam could see the woman more clearly. He saw the curve of her hip where the blue coat was cinched with a black leather belt and he saw the sharp angle of her shoulder. He saw the shiny red polish on her fingernails.

Then Sam noticed the stillness of the woman's body. It was a different stillness than he had ever seen before.

"I think she's dead," he said in a barely audible voice.

Jimmy looked at Sam and gave a derisive snort. "Sure," he said, "people come here all the time to die. It's one of their favorite places." He turned and walked up to the woman. "Hey!" he shouted. "Hey! Get up. It's time to go." When there was no response he lifted one foot and pushed his shoe against the woman's shoulder. At first he pushed gently and then he pushed hard.

"Jesus," Jimmy said. He backed away from the woman. "I think you're right, Sam. Her shoulder doesn't feel normal. It's all stiff and funny."

A light breeze ruffled some wisps of hair that fell across the woman's face.

"What do you think killed her?" asked Sam. His voice was shaking and he noticed that he was breathing fast. Suddenly, everything was running fast and slow at the same time, like when the frames of a movie get off track and the images don't quite blend together.

"How should I know," said Jimmy. "Maybe she committed suicide. Or maybe she's a whore and her pimp killed her to send a message to the others. What difference does it make?"

"I don't know. It seems like it should make a difference."

Jimmy turned and looked at his friend. "Hey," he said. "I'll give you fifty cents if you go up and touch her."

"You're crazy," Sam said.

"What are you afraid of? You think some spook is going to get you?"

"No. But it doesn't make any sense. There's no point to it."

"You're just a chicken," said Jimmy. "A goddamn chicken."

Sam looked at the woman. He tried to see her face through the tangled strands of hair but the buzzing, speeded-up feeling made it hard to concentrate. Everything seemed to be happening way too fast. It was like the night his mother told him about his father's cancer.

Without knowing that he was going to do it, Sam took a small step forward. Nothing about the woman changed in that step, nothing at all. She was still sitting quietly against the brick wall of the church, her hands folded on her lap. Then Sam took another step and again nothing changed. And then he stiffened his shoulders and walked all the way up, kneeling next to the woman on the hard wet ground.

Close now, Sam could tell that she was young, just twenty-five or so, and pretty, with a small nose and full lips. His gaze traveled along her arm to where her hands rested on her lap. They were beautiful hands, Sam thought, small and delicate, even though the color wasn't right. On the third finger of her right hand there was a silver ring with a bright blue stone.

Still looking at the woman, Sam thought about his father. His mother had said that he would soon be getting well and coming home but Sam thought she might be wrong about that. There were things in life that you could not be sure about and that was one of them. And then there was the matter of the oxygen tent. Being sick was hard enough, but being cut off from other people like that had to be a terrible thing.

Sam reached out and covered the woman's hand with his own. He felt the coldness of her skin and the slick hardness of her painted fingernails. He saw the mud stain on her shoulder where Jimmy had pushed her with his foot. His arm began to shake

At the far end of the alley, Sam faintly heard the other boys arriving for the Boy Scout meeting. He heard them call back and forth to each other and laugh. He heard Mr. Evans, the Scoutmaster, shout for them to form up in a line, and then he heard Jimmy's voice from just behind his shoulder: "I'm going to get somebody." And then he heard his friend running away on the loose gravel.

Kneeling in the parking lot, Sam held the young woman's hand. He wondered if being dead was hard and if she knew that he was there and if she took comfort from his touch. He hoped she did but he was far from certain. In any case, it didn't matter because he knew that he would stay. If he could stand it he would stay and hold the woman's hand, stay so that she wouldn't have to be alone, stay until someone came to take her away. He didn't know why, exactly, because it didn't make any sense. But it seemed like the right thing for a scout to do.

Infinite

I'm at the old Detroit ballpark one night in June when this guy claims I'm staring at his wife. He gets right out of his seat and hollers at me. This young guy with blond curly hair. "Keep your god-damned eyes to home," he says. Which was funny because I hadn't even noticed the woman sitting next to him.

The reason I'm at the ballpark is because *my* wife has just run off with her ceramics teacher and I'm looking for things to occupy my mind. Pure, simple things like baseball. Ever since Wednesday, when I got Darlene's message off the machine, I've been re-evaluating my life. Because when something like that happens to you—your wife runs off—it causes you to question things. You take a hard look at your life, and for me that's forty-seven years worth. And what I finally decided—late last night with a glass of Johnny Walker in my hand—was that I needed to make some changes. There were things about me I didn't like any more. Things that had changed me from the person I used to be. How I treated people, mainly. Darlene, included.

So I'm there at the ballpark and this young guy is standing up, looking as if he wants to fight. I glance at the woman sitting next to him; she's young, twenty-five or so, and pretty. Her hands are folded primly on her lap and she's looking out at the field as if everything is fine. A tiny smile wrinkles the corners of her mouth.

And that's when it hits me. It's the smile that gives her away. This woman isn't the guy's wife at all. She's his girl-friend. And hollering at me—who happens to be a short guy—is his way of impressing her.

I'd like to teach this guy a lesson. That's what my instincts are screaming at me to do. But I remember the vow I made and bite back the anger that's starting to pop in me like a rivet gun. Instead of getting angry I decide to play along. Because playing along will fit in with my plans to be a better person. It'll be a nice gesture, one man to another. Boost this guy in his girlfriend's eyes and make *her* feel better, too, in the bargain.

So I say to the guy, contrite: "I'm sorry, friend, I guess I got a little carried away by a pretty face." And he says, kind of gruff: "Okay, just watch it." And I say, "No hard feelings?" and he nods, sharp, and sits back down.

I give my attention back to the game. Fryman sacrifices to deep left field and then some rookie pops out to second. As the Tigers take the field I sneak a glance down the row. The guy's girlfriend, she's still staring straight ahead. But now her smile has grown a little wider, and the hand that had been folded on her lap now rests lightly on her boyfriend's knee.

And then I feel a little smile come onto *my* face too. Because by acting against my normal instincts I've moved things in a positive direction. I've made the world a better place, if only for these two people.

So I decide to take the situation one step further. I lean in the guy's direction. "Buy you a beer after the game, friend?" I say with a smile. "I'd like to make amends."

He turns and stares at me, draws his head back like he can't believe what he's hearing. Then he trades a look with his girlfriend. She's got long honey-colored hair and a small face with lively eyes. She shrugs. "Okay," he says.

"Tommy Busby," I say, putting out my hand. "Eric Dunning," he says back, and I flash him a bigger smile. "This is Rita," he says, with a wave toward his girlfriend, and I smile at Rita and touch my hand to an imaginary hat brim. It's a gesture I use with certain women.

How I make a living is that I own a car upholstery shop on Eight Mile Road. We work with car fabrics, whatever you want us to do, but mainly we replace worn-out convertible tops. That's sixty, seventy percent of our business.

We take other jobs, too, when business gets slow—non-fabric things like car alarms, custom wheels, special horns—but our favorite kind of job, what makes us the most money, is convertible tops.

When I tell my neighbors in Birmingham that I own a car upholstery shop they give me this look. I've seen it over and over again. From guys who are doctors or lawyers or executives with one of the car companies. But that little shop on Eight Mile Road has given me and Darlene a good life. It's set us up in a nice colonial with four big fluted pillars out front and a kidney-shaped pool shimmering in the back yard like a dream. I drive a white Jaguar XKE and Darlene sports around town in a midnight blue Range Rover.

At least she did until last Wednesday. Now the Range Rover is somewhere out in Colorado, if I can believe the message she left on my machine.

Anyway, when you own a small-margin business like auto upholstery you have to do certain things. It's automatic. Little presents for the health and safety inspectors, creative things on your taxes, some monkey business with insurance. Or maybe it's putting something over on a customer: passing off used hubcaps to a guy who's not too bright, or overcharging a rich old lady who doesn't know much about cars. Nothing terrible, you understand. Nothing *illegal*. But the kind of thing that makes you feel queasy at the end of the day. The kind of thing that seeps into your life and changes it, little by little.

Darlene, she saw it, too. That's why she left. She said she'd had enough of a life lived in the moral shadows—those were her words exactly. *Grubbing for money* was another term she used. She said she wanted to make a change and explore her spiritual side by working with ceramics. The spiritual side is what connects us to the infinite, she said, and I should check it out, too. "You need to take a hard look at your life, Tommy," she said on the machine. "Stop cheating people and only thinking about yourself. Make some changes and then maybe I'll come back."

So that's what I've been doing. Taking a hard look at my life and trying to be a better person. Connecting myself to the infinite, just like Darlene said. Before it's too late.

We make our way down the long concrete ramp to the street, Eric, Rita, and me, trading small talk while we crest along in the surge of disappointed Tiger fans.

"Where to?" says Eric, when we reach the street. It's the first good look I get of him. He's tall, with a big head of blond hair and a perfect set of teeth. He wears a polo shirt that shows the picture of a sailing yacht and the words: "Bring the Cup Up—Freemantle, 1992."

"I know a good place," I say, and I start to lead the way. We cross Trumbel Avenue, picking our way around potholes and jammed-up traffic, and go down a couple of dark side streets to a place I used to frequent called Hank's.

"*This* place?" says Eric. He cranes his neck to see the neon sign above the door. The H is busted so it says only "*anks*."

"It's better inside," I say.

Eric rubs his chin. I'm pretty certain he'd rather be stepping onto the deck of a racing sloop than through the doors of Hank's. "I don't know about this," he says. He surveys the littered sidewalk and the gravel parking lot, where a rusted Chevy sits up on blocks.

"Come on," says Rita, and she gives Eric's arm a friendly swat. "Don't be a party pooper." The H is starting to flicker now, making Rita's face look festive and exciting.

"That's the ticket," I say, and I push through the door before Eric can say another word.

Inside, Hank's is a little different than I remember. It's darker, for one thing, and with a new type of clientele: solitary people hunched over their drinks who don't even bother to look up when we come in. For a minute I wonder if I've made a mistake. But then I see the long mahogany bar where Norm Cash held court in '62, the big mirror spotted with yellowed news accounts of long-forgotten ball games, old black-and-white team photos thumb-tacked to the wall, and I start to feel better.

I take Rita's hand and lead her through the crowd while Eric comes along behind. We find a booth near the back and order a pitcher of Stroh's from a hefty-figured waitress who's decked out in a bright blue kimono. Then Rita gets up and excuses herself. "I've got to tinkle," she says, and disappears toward the back.

Eric and I look each other over, smiling like idiots, elbows on the table. There's family money and a first-rate education written all over him. He's the kind of guy who takes success for granted. Whose bill I'd pad with an extra hundred dollar charge if he came into my shop. I picture him in Freemantle—wherever that is—hoisting up a beer with his fraternity brothers, toasting the success of a million-dollar yacht.

"I want to apologize for what happened back there in the stadium," he says. "It was a stupid trick."

"Oh," I say, coy.

"Yeah," he says. "I thought we'd trade some angry words and I'd end up looking like a big shot to Rita. Defending her honor and all."

"That's what I thought," I say.

"No hard feelings?" he says.

"Course not," I say. But then, a few seconds later, I add: "Just one thing. Was it my size that made you pick me?"

"What do you mean?"

"Me being a short guy. That you thought you could beat up."

He shrugs, looks a little uncomfortable. "I don't know. Maybe."

"Because if that's what you thought, you'd be wrong."

He shrugs again. "So what?" he says.

"Nothing," I say. "I just want you to know."

Eric sits up a little straighter and folds his arms across his chest. We stare at each other over the worn Formica, two guys from opposite sides of the tracks sizing each other up. I've got to admit that I like what's happening. Facing down big guys is sort of a specialty of mine. I do it every day in my business. The fact that Eric is young and rich and has a pretty girlfriend is just a bonus.

I'm thinking I'd like to take things to the next level—that's the level where I ask Eric if he wants to step outside—but all of a sudden I remember Darlene and my new resolution. I laugh out loud and pat Eric's arm. "Had you going there," I say to him.

"Yeah," he says. He grins sheepishly and rubs one cheek.

Just then Rita comes back. She's freshened herself up, dabbed on a little make-up. As she hunches herself into the booth, I get a good whiff of perfume, something flowery and nice. I pour Rita a beer and flash a big smile. She smiles right back, no hesitation.

We talk for a while, getting to know each other. Eric is a lawyer in his father's law firm—no big surprise there—and Rita is a receptionist for an optometrist that makes eyeglasses in one hour.

"That's how we met," Rita says, and she gives a shy sideways glance at Eric. "We work in the same building. He's upstairs and I'm down."

"That's real interesting," I say, although I'm wondering how much a lawyer and an eyeglass receptionist can have in common. "How do they do that anyway?" I ask. Rita turns her lively eyes on me. "Make those glasses in just one hour."

"It's technology," Eric says, before Rita has a chance to answer. He leans forward like he's afraid I won't hear him. "Optical technology and special lens materials. Polycarbons. The Japanese developed it."

I give him a hard stare. "You don't say."

"Yeah," he says, smiling.

❄   ❄   ❄

The reason I know about Hank's is that I used to go there when I followed baseball. This was before I married Darlene, back when I was just starting up my car upholstery business and still living at home with my folks. In those days most of the games were played in the afternoon and afterwards some of the players would stop by Hank's for a little refreshment. They'd have a couple of beers and if they knew you—if you were a regular like me—they'd let you join in. It was mostly the new players who went there, the young ones struggling to break in from the minors; but that was fine with me because I was sort of a new guy, too—in the auto fabric business, I mean.

Back then, I probably loved baseball more than anything else in the world. To me, a baseball stadium was a place where everything was damn near perfect: the grass, the smooth white sand along the base paths, the trueness of the foul lines. And there was something else I liked about it, too: an orderliness I guess you'd call it, a sense of how things could work in a better world. Because whenever I got discouraged, or angry at some guy who was trying to take advantage of me, I would think about the baseball park and get myself calmed down. It was the only place I knew where all the rules were fair, all the consequences known.

Growing up in Detroit, Harvey Kuenn was my hero. I liked his moves at second base and I liked the fact he was the batting champ for four years running. Back then, twelve years old, I wanted to be a shortstop, too. You know how your mind works when you're a kid: you just decide a thing and figure it's going to happen. Later on you learn there's more to it. A lot more. There's such things as talent and opportunity. And being too short. And knowing who the right people are. But for a while you live in a make-believe world, a state of bliss, where anything is possible.

The first thing that happened to change that feeling was when Kuenn got traded to the Indians. It was one of the all-time lousy baseball deals—something hatched in a back room between rich guys drunk with power—and it rocked the baseball world. I suppose you remember it, too: Kuenn for Coliveto, one-for-one, batting champion for home run king.

And it rocked my world, too. For two days I didn't come out of my bedroom, didn't go to school, didn't eat a thing. Just stayed behind my locked door ignoring my mother's pleas and my father's threats. Thinking.

And crying.

When I finally did come out things were different and they always would be. In Brooklyn they talk about when the Dodgers moved to L.A.: that was what broke their hearts and made them understand how the world really worked. In Detroit it was the Kuenn for Coliveto trade of 1960.

"What's your line of work," Eric says to me.

We've been at Hank's for about an hour and things are rolling along pretty good. I've learned that Rita likes Humphrey Bogart movies, same as me. And she wants to be a fashion model—if she had her choice—which is sort of in the category of my old shortstop aspirations. Now that Darlene has gone off to Colorado to do ceramics I'm thinking that maybe I should get to know some other women, and this Rita might be a good place to start.

Over at the bar some guys are laughing and talking loud. They've livened it up and made it seem more like the old days. A whoop rings out that causes me to look in their direction. A husky guy in a Hawaiian shirt breaks away from the crowd and begins to dance, that Greek dance that Anthony Quinn did in the movie, hands over his head and snapping his fingers. The others laugh and clap.

I turn back to Eric and Rita and I begin to tell them about my car upholstery business. For some reason I'm still smarting about what happened in the stadium, Eric's challenge and then telling me it was because of my size. All night I've been pretending it didn't matter, but deep down I feel a little wound. So I lay it on thick, describe my house in Birmingham, the fluted columns, the pool, the albino tiger I petted on vacation once in Mazatlán. I see Rita eye my sapphire ring.

"You married, Tom?" Eric asks me.

"Yeah," I say. "But my wife's not exactly with me right now." I force out a tiny smile.

"What do you mean?" asks Eric.

"My wife ran off to Colorado with some guy."

"Oh, poor baby," Rita says. She leans forward and touches the back of my hand like she's petting a favorite tiny animal. I take her fingers and look straight into her pale blue eyes. I have the definite feeling something is going to happen here, or *could* happen if I wanted it to.

"Yeah. It's tough," I say. Her hand is warm as toast.

"Because I was just wondering," she continues. She smiles and shows a line of perfect teeth. "A nice guy like you. At the ballpark alone."

I give Rita's hand a friendly squeeze and her smile grows wider. A moment passes; and then, at the fuzzy edges of my vision, I detect some movement. Eric shifts in his seat, realigns his arms and elbows. Suddenly Rita's hand disappears like smoke.

"We should probably go now," Eric says. "I've got a big day tomorrow in court." He starts to rise.

"Hold on!" I say. I reach up and grasp his arm.

I want to make them stay—at least until I can get Rita's phone number—and so I say something I've been saving up since we came in.

"Do you know what this bar is famous for?"

Eric slumps back down. "No," he says. "I don't."

I grin. "This is the bar where Lou Gehrig came after he took himself out of the lineup." I look across the table, waiting for their reactions. "He came over here from the stadium and listened to the game on the radio while he ate a ham sandwich and drank a beer. May 2, 1939."

"Oh," says Rita.

"It was before my time, of course," I say. "But things like that don't get forgotten."

"Did he play for the Tigers?" says Eric.

I look at him. "Lou Gehrig!" I say.

They stare back at me.

"Two thousand, one-hundred, and thirty straight games," I say.

Rita and Eric trade looks. Then Eric shrugs and offers up a sloppy smile.

"Never mind," I say, with a disgusted backhand wave.

"Tell me about him," says Eric.

"It's not important," I say.

"Oh, pweese," says Rita. She's picked up on my sour mood and has decided to joke me out of it. Plus I think she's a little drunk. "Pweese tell us."

I lift my glass and take a long slow swallow. Then I look across the room. The man at the bar—the one who had been dancing—has removed his Hawaiian shirt. He's turned to show his bare back to his friends. Just above a pointy collarbone is the purple splash of a tattoo. It sits against his eggshell skin like a large but harmless bug. I squint through cigarette haze and see the figure of a naked lady on a clamshell.

"He was a famous Yankee first baseman," I say, still looking at the man with the tattoo. "Then he got sick and couldn't play baseball any more."

There's silence as Eric and Rita take in this information.

"Oh, yeah," says Eric, finally. "I think I remember seeing a movie about that."

"*Pride of the Yankees,*" I say. "With Gary Cooper."

Eric purses his lips and nods in a serious way, as if he's seeing through to the core of some complicated argument.

"The thing is," I continue, " he didn't have to do it." The tattooed guy is buttoning his shirt now. "It was his own choice to take himself out of the game. Because he knew he wasn't up to playing any more."

I look at Rita. She smiles back encouragingly and nods her head. "He knew it was hopeless," I add.

"That's wery interesting," says Rita, still nodding. "Wery, wery."

I take off my glasses and rub my eyes. Nothing is turning out the way I expected it to. Eric and Rita are smiling at me across a tabletop littered with pretzel crumbs and bright puddles of beer. Their round faces seem to float like a constellation in the dim universe of Hank's. They're young and beautiful and I recognize their shared expression: it's the wide-eyed look of people trying to understand what they've gotten themselves into.

I feel the cool blur of a tear on my left cheek. Hurriedly, I wipe it away.

"Easy there, old buddy," says Eric. I feel his hand on my forearm.

"For heaven's sake," says Rita. Through my blurred vision I see her make a quick circuit of the room to see if anyone is noticing me. Then she tips her head down in embarrassment, one flat hand shielding her eyes.

"Geez, Rita," says Eric. "Can't you see Tom is feeling bad about Lou Greg." He turns to me. "Buck up, Tom. I'll bet that didn't even happen here. I'll bet the bar where that old guy went was torn down a long time ago."

I feel the steady pressure of Eric's hand on my arm. It's the sweet consoling gesture of a nice guy. I push his hand away.

❊   ❊   ❊

It's late now. No one has spoken for quite a while. Across the table, Eric rolls up the corner of a napkin, then flattens it out. Rita nods her head in time to some internal rhythm. She seems to have gotten over her embarrassment at my little show; at least I hope she has.

"That about those eye glasses is interesting," I say to her, trying to spark a little conversation.

"Yeah," Rita says, and sighs. "I guess so." Then: "Too bad about your wife."

"Those things happen," I say.

"Still," she says, and breaths out another sigh.

Her hands are folded on the tabletop and her gaze is lowered as if she's contemplating something deep and sentimental. For a moment I examine a tiny scar that puckers the skin above her right eyebrow.

"Well....," Eric says. He pushes himself into a standing position. "We really have to go now." He makes a sign to Rita and she scoots out of the booth. As she does she slides a slip of paper in my direction. I palm it quickly.

"Thanks for the hospitality," Eric says. He reaches down to shake my hand.

"Don't mention it," I say. Then I add: "I'll guess I'll have to behave myself better next time I go to the ball park."

"Yeah," Eric says, and we both laugh because it's like a private joke we have between us.

"It's been a real pleasure," Rita says, primlike, putting out her hand. I take it and smile, and then for fun I give her a wink, but by accident both my eyes close together. I decide to let it go at that, let Rita take whatever meaning she can get.

The next thing I know, Rita and Eric have pushed out through the swinging door and I'm sitting all alone at Hank's. I open up my hand. Resting in the center of my palm is the torn-off corner of a napkin—soggy from beer or perspiration—with a phone number scrawled on it. I hesitate for a moment, then carefully fold the napkin and put it into my wallet.

I look around the bar, hoping I'll find another group to join up with. But Hank's is almost empty now—even the guy with the Hawaiian shirt has disappeared—and an eerie stillness has settled over the place. It's not a normal silence, either; at least it doesn't feel normal to me. It seems to have weight and physical dimensions, and it bears down and holds me like an insect fixed between two panes of glass. And then I recognize it's the deafening silence of bygone years and bygone aspirations, things long dead that I still cling to, things I can't escape.

Reluctantly I stand and head for the door.

Outside, the summer nighttime air has turned cool. A layer of dew has settled onto the ground, covering the candy wrappers and cigarette butts with a silvery glaze. Above me the neon H blinks crazily.

Off in the distance I see Rita and Eric walking to their car. A streetlamp sweeps their giant shadows across a building wall, then Rita half-stumbles and Eric reaches out and grabs her arm. "Steady, sweetie," he says. She laughs and they turn a corner.

I start walking in the opposite direction, up toward the old stadium that I know so well. A gentle breeze moves air against my face; brick walls bounce back my solitary footsteps. I think about Darlene and the vow I've made and broken that very day, the one she doesn't even know about. I picture her atop a stool in some potter's shed in Colorado, shaping mounds of clay, searching for the infinite. I can't help wondering if *we'll* ever make our unsteady way down a littered street again, or any kind of street at all. I hope we will but I'm far from certain. If not, I guess I'll still have Rita's slip of paper in my wallet.

Up ahead, the sheltering left field wall comes into view. It looms above me, a straight gray slab shooting up one hundred feet or more. Its size is startling, and puts me in mind of some national monument, or the sharp boundary between warring nations.

I crane my neck so I can see it better. Overhead, a gauzy quarter moon shoots down its glow among a random spray of brilliant stars. I reach up and place my hand against the cool gray mass and offer up a prayer. I mean for it to go to God, but in my mind I picture Lou Gehrig sitting at Hank's, a ham sandwich in one hand.

That's the best that I can do.

A siren wails in some far-off corner of the city, and, then, closer, I hear the urgent barking of a dog. The infinite is out there, just like Darlene says, but it's not going to connect to me.

Not tonight, anyway.

Bypass

Frank Gallespie stood at his front window at noon waiting for his ex-wife Sylvia. It was a snowy November day. Outside, the neighborhood kids were running around his yard, catching snowflakes in their mouths, yelling and carrying on as if it—the snow—were a new concept that had been invented for their sole enjoyment. The way they looked out there—heads tilted back, mouths agape, pink tongues extended into the frozen air—reminded Frank of little birds demanding to be fed by the mamma bird. Frank seemed to remember his own kids doing the same thing years and years ago; catching snowflakes in your mouth, a stupid kid thing to do, nothing else.

Frank was feeling edgy. He wished the kids would go away and make their racket someplace else. He'd been out of the hospital for only one week after having a bypass operation, and he was still trying to deal with the feelings the experience had stirred up in him. His doctor, a sandy-haired young man who could have been Frank's son, had assured him the operation had turned out fine—*splendid* was the word he had actually used—but Frank wondered if anyone could really know about such things. If the operation had not turned out fine would the sandy-haired doctor have told him? Or would Frank even know himself? He supposed a person could lose some quality—drift into a world less sharp, less vivid, less *interesting*—and not even know it. Frank was sixty-two and not ready to give up. He still wanted to prove himself, although he couldn't say in what way exactly.

Outside, a dark blue Cadillac turned the corner and started down the street. It came fast, fishtailing wildly in the deep snow, the rear tires spitting up plumes of white. Even if his ex-wife Sylvia had not called that morning to announce that she was coming for a visit, Frank might have guessed it was her behind the wheel. That heedless approach to driving—and to everything else she did these days—was her style completely. Taking for granted that everybody would stay out of her way. As if she owned the goddamned road. Frank knew all about it.

The big car lumbered up into the driveway. At the same moment, something like a restless garter snake began to coil inside Frank's stomach. His last clear rec-

ollection of Sylvia centered on an argument they'd had
six months ago in the corridor of the Oakland County
Courthouse. Kneeling on a marble floor while the
judge waited in his chamber they had divided the collection of lighthouse photos from their 1986 vacation
to New Brunswick, for some odd reason the last un-
accounted property they owned in common. Neither
of them had actually cared much for New Brunswick
and its gray, dispiriting landscape, or for lighthouses
for that matter, or even photography; but they had
been driven by principle, neither being willing—after
twenty-three years—to surrender any portion of their
marital rights.

It had only required three months; that was all the time
it took to go from being a relatively happy married couple
to the bitterest of enemies. Frank had set things in motion
by suddenly finding fault with qualities in Sylvia that had
remained unchanged for years, from the offhand way
she dressed (Frank began to call it sloppy) to her habit,
when excited, of starting every sentence twice. It was as
if on hitting a certain age Frank could no longer tolerate
his wife's smallest imperfections, or at least his cramped
version of them. He was an architect, after all, and he
had all the megalomania of that profession. The perfect
structures he created each day on paper needed suddenly
to be matched—in a sort of final test of professional wor-
thiness—by the features of his own life.

Of course his campaign had failed. Feeling set upon, Sylvia demanded that Frank get rid of the vintage Mercedes that had been undergoing reconstruction in their garage since 1986, and that he stop playing the marching band music that he liked to listen to at night. And then—Frank couldn't remember exactly how it happened—the situation took a sinister turn, as each day Sylvia discovered fresh sources of outrage, like powerful subterranean currents that had suddenly been tapped. She had, by her telling, forsaken many worthy opportunities to marry Frank, put the brakes on a budding real estate career to stay at home with the kids, sat alone countless nights while Frank was off at conferences or entertaining clients, and circumscribed their social life to the dour crew of Frank's associates. Their disagreements—which had been benign and even comical—suddenly became ugly; and then the word divorce was uttered and lawyers were on the scene.

What happened next was still a blur. Under the watchful eyes of various well-intentioned counselors, Frank and Sylvia were persuaded they had little in the way of common interests, to acknowledge the hopelessness of such a situation, and to untangle the lives they had built together for so long. Like embarrassed children caught perpetrating some unsavory deception, they sorted out their personal effects, split their bank accounts into equal shares, and made arrangements to go their separate ways. Frank, it was decided, would stay on in the house, and Sylvia (who was always more adaptable) would set herself up in one of the spanking new apartments on the edge of town.

The altercation about the lighthouse photos—Frank understood this now—had been the last wrenching gasp of a marriage that should never have happened.

Sylvia stepped out onto the snowy driveway, a big casserole dish clutched in her hands. She bumped the car door closed with a little sashay of her hip and headed up the walk, stepping gingerly with high heels in the freshly fallen snow. Halfway to the door she spotted the neighbor kids—still going crazy in Frank's front yard—and yelled something in their direction. The kids stopped their antics and gave her an appraising look, obviously contemplating some insult or retaliation. But then they turned and ran off down the street.

"Hey," Frank said, holding open the front door. "Look who's come for a visit."

"Hi, Frankie," Sylvia said. She stepped up into the little vestibule and stomped her feet. Bits of snow flew onto the flagstone floor like confetti.

"Did you come back for the rest of the lighthouse photos?"

Sylvia threw a sharp glance in Frank's direction. "Don't get started with that, Frank. That's a road we don't want to go down." She glared at him for a moment, but then she smiled sweetly and held out the casserole. "Besides, this is a mission of mercy," she said, "not a shakedown."

Frank took the offering, peering at it skeptically.

"Don't worry," Sylvia said. She began to remove her

coat. "It's only a tuna casserole, not poison. I made extra last night."

"Thanks," Frank said. "I guess I can use it." He nodded through the open door. "Nice car," he said.

"It's a loaner from Bernie." Sylvia said. She closed the door and headed toward the living room. "Mine's in the shop."

Frank carried the casserole into the kitchen and set it on the counter. He had no idea who Bernie was and he had no intention of asking. Since their divorce, Sylvia always seemed to be receiving favors from men whose names were unfamiliar to Frank. Likewise, she had no trouble finding companions to escort her to the art and charity functions that had become a part of her new routine. There had even been some talk—although Frank dismissed it as spurious—of a weekend in Chicago with someone named Bud.

"What'd you say to those kids?" Frank asked, returning to the living room. Sylvia had thrown her coat across a chair and was examining a cluster of medicines arranged on the coffee table.

"What?" She picked up a bottle and held it toward the light, examining the label.

"Those kids out there. You said something and they ran away."

"It wasn't anything important." She set the bottle down. "I just said there was a sick person who lived in the house and for them to go and make their racket someplace else."

Frank felt the little snake move in his stomach. He was

trying hard not to think of himself as *sick*, exactly, even though deep down he understood that certain things had changed in a permanent way. He was learning to live with the sensation, familiar to arctic explorers and Michigan ice fishermen, of being supported by a fragile membrane, camped out on a crust of ice above a cold, black void.

But more than his health it was the state of his own life that worried Frank these days. In contrast to Sylvia, he had made few changes after the divorce: he'd stayed on at the architectural firm, continued to spend his evenings tinkering with the Mercedes and listening to his marching bands, and faithfully attended the weekly meetings of the Model Railroaders' Club, for which he served this year as Treasurer. But now he was beginning to think this lack of change evidenced a defect in his make-up. More than anything, he wanted to assert himself, to show that he still mattered, to take charge of things in the way he'd felt in charge when they'd been married.

Frank waved Sylvia toward the leather sofa while he took a seat in the La-Z-Boy, lowering himself slowly so as not to strain the line of sutures neatly bisecting his chest.

"I can only stay a few minutes," Sylvia said. "I've got a house showing at one."

"That's okay. I usually take a nap after lunch, anyway."

"I came by the hospital after the operation, but the nurses said you were still out from the anesthetic. I left some flowers and a funny card."

"I got them," Frank said. "Thanks."

"I was worried about you, Frankie. But I didn't know if you wanted to see me. So soon after the divorce and all."

"Oh," he said, "I think it would have been fine."

Sylvia smiled at him across the living room. Despite himself, Frank was struck by how good she looked. She had always been a shorter woman and a little on the heavy side, but Frank had to admit that today she looked quite nice. Her stylish blue dress made her appear almost delicate, and the silk scarf clinging to her shoulders seemed to float there like a colorful cloud. She reminded Frank of photographs in the AARP magazine he had recently started to read—the ones that showed older couples having fun together and keeping up their interests.

"What do you do to make the time pass?" Sylvia asked. She had kicked off her damp shoes and tucked her feet up under her. The bright blue dress inched up, revealing a section of her thigh.

"I've got a routine," Frank said, keeping his gaze on Sylvia's face. "The doctor gave me some weights to do arm exercises with. Four times a day. And there's a plastic tube I breath through to build up my lungs."

Sylvia made a sour face and immediately Frank wished he could take back his remarks. The last thing he wanted was to become a comic spectacle or an object of her pity. He gave a lopsided smile, as if to acknowledge the absurd state he'd temporarily fallen into. Then he decided to steer the conversation in a new direction.

"You remember that time we were in Charlevoix and went cross-country skiing back in the woods?" he asked.

"And there was that dog running loose. That German Shepherd or whatever it was."

Sylvia touched a finger to the corner of her mouth. "I guess so," she said. Then: "What made you think of that, Frankie? That was a long time ago."

"I guess the snow made me remember. I've been thinking I might like to do some cross-country skiing again. Maybe in a few weeks when I feel better."

Sylvia stared at him, saying nothing.

"I might do some traveling, too," he continued. "To Kenya or Turkey. Maybe Morocco. I've always wanted to see Tangiers."

A little frown crept onto Sylvia's face. "Do you think that's a good idea, Frankie? To go off to those faraway places in your condition."

"Why not?" he said. "My hearts all fixed now." He tapped his chest.

Sylvia looked at him for a moment as if she were unconvinced. "Well, anyway," she said, "it sounds like plenty of fun. I remember you used to talk about traveling some day, but I always thought you meant just the U.S. of A."

Frank smiled at Sylvia, feeling better about the way the conversation was going. He was beginning to feel a little more like his old self—making plans and anticipating events—and Sylvia—perched there on the sofa with her feet tucked up under her—was beginning to remind him of the old Sylvia, the one who could be sweet and interesting.

"Why don't you stick around and have some of that tuna casserole with me," Frank offered.

Sylvia wrinkled her forehead and stared hard at the floor in a parody of concentration.

"I guess the real estate market won't crash if I'm gone for a little while," she said with a bright smile.

"That's the spirit," Frank said.

Sylvia unfolded herself from the sofa and headed into the kitchen. Frank heard the radio come on, the sound of rustling in the cupboards, dishes clanking together, pots being handled. After a few minutes she returned carrying two bowls of tuna casserole. "Here, Frank," she said. "*Bon appétit.*"

They sat and ate the tuna casserole—Sylvia's tuna casserole—and talked about their children: Angela in law school in Indiana; Sam teaching at the inner-city school in Philadelphia. A television set played softly in the corner and during the pauses in the conversation they looked at it distractedly. Frank had it tuned to a game show where contestants answered embarrassing questions or else got dropped into a vat of green slime. Each time the bell went off to announce the trap door was about to open, Sylvia emitted a tiny gasp.

"I guess you're doing pretty well with the real estate stuff," Frank said, after a while.

"Not bad, I guess," Sylvia said. "I got a bonus last month for selling the most in our office."

"I suppose it's a lot better than staying home."

"I like it," she said. "It's different and exciting. But I

liked being home, too, Frankie. Having all that time to think and read."

"That's not what you said in the divorce papers."

Sylvia laughed briefly. "All that stuff at the end, Frankie, it was just lawyer's talk. You know that. "

"You said some pretty mean things—about the Mercedes and the band music."

"And you didn't, I suppose."

Frank shrugged. What did it matter? All of that was in the past. It was the future Frank needed to think about now, how he was going to build an interesting life with a patched-up heart—and without the woman he'd lived with for twenty-three years.

Frank turned his head and looked out the window. The snow was coming down harder now, fat, slow-drifting flakes that were starting to blanket the blue Cadillac. He thought about the life he'd shared with Sylvia, the life they'd torn apart just six months ago. They might not have been a model couple, or even shared many interests, but they had cared about each other. Somehow, in spite of all the obstacles, they had managed that. They'd loved each other; in their own peculiar way they had. That was something Frank was sure of.

Frank turned back to Sylvia. He set the bowl of tuna casserole on the side table and ratcheted his La-Z-Boy into the forward position.

"I've been thinking about some things, Sylvia," he announced.

"Oh." Her eyebrows arched over the top of her bowl.

"What things, Frankie?"

Frank cast around in his mind for the words to express how he felt about her. There was so much he wanted to tell her, so much he should have said long ago, so much he hadn't been able to say during the last horrible months of their marriage. And there were other things, too, that he wanted to reveal: things that only Sylvia would understand. He wanted to tell her his doubts about the doctor's hopeful statements, and the black thoughts that came to him in the middle of the night, and the frightening sensation of always living on a crust of ice.

Frank looked at Sylvia, his mind clogged with thoughts. He couldn't talk about everything—they'd be there all day—but he had to make a start.

"I'm going to have a scar, Sylvia," he said.

She blinked a few times, saying nothing.

"Right down the center of my chest."

Sylvia moved her gaze onto Frank's chest, then back to his face. "So what?" she said.

Frank hesitated, wondering if he was making a mistake.

"So I'm going to have to wear shirts all the time. I can't ever go bare-chested again. Not even in summer."

Sylvia looked at him with a slightly puzzled expression. "That'd be too bad," she said, speaking hesitantly. "And you've got such a nice chest, too, Frank." She forked up some tuna casserole, sucking the loose end of a noodle into her mouth. Then her eyes narrowed slightly, as if she were going through some kind of internal calculation.

"Let's see it," she said.

"What?"

"Let's see the scar."

"I don't think that's a good idea, Sylvia."

"Why not, Frankie? We're all adults here."

Frank shrugged. He sat forward in the La-Z-Boy and began to unbutton his shirt, working each bit of plastic through its tiny hole. When the last button came undone he hesitated for a moment. Then he pulled the shirt open.

At first Sylvia didn't say anything. She simply stared at Frank's chest with a slightly pinched expression, like a person feeling the first faint throb of a migraine, or witnessing a car accident that might include fatalities. Seeing her expression, Frank thought again that he'd made a terrible mistake. Out of all the subjects he could have chosen to talk about, the scar was clearly the wrong one.

A moment passed. Frank held his breath. Finally, Sylvia's expression softened. She curled her lip and blew a wisp of hair out of her eyes.

"I guess I see your point," she said, speaking in a thoughtful voice. "But it'll heal up some more, Frank. That's the first thing you should remember. Plus you can always wear tee shirts. If you go to the beach or whatever. Tee shirts that show off your shape."

"I hadn't thought about that," he said.

"The shape is the main thing anyway," she said. "People don't need to know what it looks like underneath."

Frank started to button up his shirt. He wasn't sure it would be as simple as Sylvia made it seem. But on the other hand, he didn't really care. The important thing wasn't the scar, after all. That was just a subject he'd grabbed onto to get the ball rolling with Sylvia, to open up a kind of channel so that they could talk about those other things.

"You've got to remember, Frank, that you're an architect."

He was standing, tucking his shirttail into his pants. "What?"

"You've got that perfectionist streak in you, Frank. That thing that goes crazy when something isn't exactly right. Let's face it, the visual part of you is stronger than in most people. Like how you used to get upset about the way I dressed and kept the house." She leaned forward and set the empty bowl onto the coffee table. "That's why it was never destined to work out between us. Even after twenty-three years. You're a literalist and I'm a figurative. That means we live in different orbits." She raised her index fingers and drew a series of tiny circles in the air. "Just like the marriage counselors said."

Frank finished tucking in his shirttail and sat back down. He looked into Sylvia's face, hoping to find there the familiar comic look that accompanied her more outrageous statements. After twenty-three years he was an expert on all of her looks, together with how they matched her many varied moods. But the look he saw now was different than any he'd seen before—intense, committed, fearless—and with a start he realized it was the look that went with her new life.

"Listen, Frank," Sylvia said. "I've got to run. If I hurry I can still make that one o'clock showing." She reached for her coat, motioning for Frank to stay in his chair. "But I'll be back in a few days. We can talk some more about your trip to Morocco, or wherever it was you said you wanted to go. I promise."

Sylvia threaded her arms into the sleeves of her coat, then came over and kissed Frank quickly on the mouth. "Just because…." She stared at him from a distance of three inches, her face enormous. "I mean, even though we're not married any more doesn't mean we can't talk to each other, right?"

Frank heard the car engine start, the crunch of tires moving over the snow, followed by the little ticks and murmurs of an empty house.

Sylvia's visit had tired him out, but it had given him much to think about.

He leaned back in his La-Z-Boy, tilting it as far as it would go, until he was in the position of an astronaut in a space capsule.

He couldn't kid himself. He would probably never have her back. Things had gone too far in a new direction for that to happen now. But at least he had opened up a channel; they had made a slight connection, something that hadn't been there for a long time.

And they could keep on talking, just like Sylvia had said. There was nothing wrong with talking. He had opened up a channel and someday—who could say?— she might come around. And in the meantime? Well, what he needed most was to match that look of hers, that look that was manifested in the heedless way she drove a car, and fought for photographs that were rightly hers, and looked at scars without flinching, and received favors, without embarrassment, from men with names like Bernie and Bud.

Frank settled himself more deeply into his chair. As had become his recent habit, he moved his hand to the center of his chest where he detected, deep within, the reassuring buck and shudder of his imperfect heart. He was sliding down toward sleep now—he could feel it coming—but before yielding he turned his head and looked once more out onto the snowy landscape.

Outside, everything was peaceful and white, startlingly white, with the exception of the spot where Sylvia's Cadillac had stood, where a black smudge of asphalt showed through the accumulating snow. Frank stared at the somber spot for a very long moment, as if it held the answer to some fascinating puzzle that had long eluded him, and then he shifted his gaze and looked off further down the street. There, several houses away, he saw the neighborhood kids. They seemed to be gathering again, talking among themselves, casting glances in his direction, as if preparing to make a fresh assault on his front yard.

Frank closed his eyes. He wasn't worried about the kids now, or anything else. For the first time in many months he felt fearless and resolved. And then he thought of Sylvia, and of Turkey and Tangiers, and of the exhilarating sense of living on a crust of ice, and of not knowing what would happen next. And then from some place far below he seemed to feel the shuddering of a rocket, a gathering force preparing to catapult him into an unknown time and space, a towering plume of smoke propelling him across the winter sky.

Curmudgeon

I had crossed the bridge and was making my way along Highway 28 to close down my summer place on Lake Superior when I spotted this woman and little boy standing alongside the road. It was early November and sleet peppered the air. The sun was just a vague white ball, low in the sky, and the weather was raw in that way that is unique to the Upper Peninsula of Michigan, as if the air still carried a vein of arctic malice left over from the glaciers that covered the area not so many millennia ago. This woman and her boy stood with their backs to the blowing wind, shoulders hunched, heads bowed, like cattle sheltering in a field. She was large; big in a muscular way—stout, I suppose you'd call her—and she wore a red down-filled jacket. The little fellow looked to be about seven years old; he was covered in a green plastic bag with a hole where his head poked through. The woman had her thumb out.

Of course I stopped. Who wouldn't? A woman and young boy along the highway with night coming on. Plus, I liked the idea of having some company for a few miles. It'd been a long, lonely drive up from Saginaw and someone to talk to—anyone at all—would be a blessing.

I guided the Bonneville onto the gravel shoulder and the woman ran up. She said she needed to get to a phone to call her sister in Munising and asked if I would take her up to the next gas station. She had a nice looking face, this woman, bright, intelligent eyes, and cheeks with dimples that looked like they could hold pennies.

I told her to climb aboard and she settled herself into the front seat while the little fellow clambered into the back. After I'd pulled back onto the highway she introduced herself: her name was Nicole, she said, and her boy's name was Brody. She'd had an argument with her boyfriend and he'd left them there alongside the highway.

"Dwayne stopped the car and told us to get out." She spoke in a matter-of-fact voice, as if being abandoned along a lonely stretch of road was a normal part of her existence. "He said we were holding him back from realizing his potential." She stopped talking for a moment while she picked a dead leaf off her sleeve and flicked it onto the floor. "He's an artist," she continued. "An artist-welder. He works with metal; that's his media."

I listened to what Nicole said and put a few things together. I've summered in the U.P. since Delores and I got married—that's almost forty-five years now—so I know these north country people pretty well. Some of them are just latter-day hippies as far as I can tell, living on food stamps and growing marijuana under Glo-Lamps in the bedroom. I know because I've hired them to do projects around my summer place: tried to, anyway, because half the time they don't show up.

"I can't imagine someone doing such a terrible thing," I said to Nicole.

"Well you've got a lot to learn, then, mister," Nicole said, laughing. "Dwayne's just crazy sometimes. But you can't completely blame him. It's his artistic temperament coming out."

"I'm cold, Mommy," Brody said from the back seat. He had a tiny voice that you could barely hear.

I reached across and cranked up the heater. Hot air began to blow around our feet. "There," I said. "We'll get you warmed up now, Brody."

"Thanks," Nicole said. She touched my arm where it rested on the steering wheel.

"Think nothing of it," I said.

Nicole was a talker. Which was okay with me, because, like I said before, I craved the company. With Delores dead three years now, and my son, Scott, run off to find his future in California, it seems like I've got too much silence in my life these days. I go to church every Sunday, just like when Delores was alive, and I see a lot of my old friends there, but during the week the days just drag. Sometimes the loneliness gets so deep I'll leave the radio on just to fill the house with sound, or I'll order something by phone from a mail-order house so I can trade a few pleasant sentences with another human soul. I've got more gardening tools and Gore-Tex windbreakers than I'll ever use in two lifetimes.

Anyway, I learned from Nicole that she was thirty-seven and a part-time hairdresser who sold Amway on the side. She'd been through two marriages, had had a number of boyfriends, plus a couple of relationships that didn't seem to fit in any particular category, at least none that I was familiar with. She'd been living with her latest boyfriend—Dwayne, who'd left her on the road—for going onto seven months.

"Any chance of marriage?" I asked.

"What? With Dwayne you mean? Maybe in a million years, but probably not before. And that's a blessing after what he did today."

Nicole took a pack of Marlboros out of her coat pocket and asked if she could smoke. I told her to go ahead and she shook one out, then lit it with a match.

"I like to keep second-hand smoke away from Brody," she said. She extinguished the match with a snap of her wrist, then cranked the window down halfway. A blast of cold air hit the back of my neck. "You wouldn't believe what they say about second-hand smoke."

We drove for a few miles without seeing much of anything. It was full dark now and we were about the only car on the road; all you could see were the ghostly shapes of pine trees flashing by the side windows and the bright throw of our headlights reaching out to grab the road in front.

"What do you think about the second amendment?" Nicole asked, all of a sudden. Just a subject out of no-where. "That's what me and Dwayne were arguing about when he put us out."

"I guess I don't think about it much, Nicole," I said. "I don't own any guns."

"Me, neither," she said. She blew a stream of smoke that got sucked away by the window crack. "Dwayne is always going on about the second amendment. How the government has a secret plan to confiscate everybody's guns, etcetera, etcetera, etcetera. I just wondered if you had an opinion about that."

"I know some people who shouldn't have a gun no matter what," I said.

"So you'd be in favor of registration, then."

"Sure," I said. "Why not?"

"What about gun shows?"

"What about them?"

"That's another facet of the problem that worries Dwayne. He thinks gun show regulation is the beginning of the slip-pery slope. You should have an opinion on that, too."

"I guess I don't understand that aspect too well," I said. "I'll defer to you there, Nicole."

"That's an abnegation of your democratic duty," Nicole said, and laughed. "Not an option." She reached forward and crushed her cigarette hard into the ashtray. A thin curl of smoke rose lazily in the green glow of the instrument panel, then disappeared. "But just in case anyone asks, I'm for instant background checks. I don't care what Dwayne says."

"That makes sense," I said. Up ahead a Mobil sign loomed up. "Sign me up for instant background checks, too." And I laughed out loud and so did Nicole.

Me and Brody stayed in the car while Nicole went into the Mobil station to call her sister in Munising. I watched through the window as a scrawny kid in grease-stained overalls counted change into Nicole's palm, then said something into her ear that made her roll her eyes.

I'll be honest. I was beginning to like Nicole. She had a manner about her that was warm and lively, and I respected the spunky way she responded to misfortune and how she had her own opinions about things. Delores—God rest her soul—was a small woman who was careful in social situations. She liked to know who she was making friends with before she opened up; which is a good way to conduct yourself, of course, when you're a Christian lady. But I could see that Nicole's way had merit, too, and was probably more fun.

"Do you live around here, mister?" It was Brody's voice from the back seat.

I turned around. Brody was crouched in the corner, his long blond hair matted to his forehead.

"No," I said. "I live downstate."

"What are you doing up here then?" Light from the rotating Mobil sign danced over the plastic sheet, giving Brody a slightly festive look.

"I have a summer home on Lake Superior."

"You mean you own two houses?"

"I guess you could say that. One is for summer and one is for winter. Only I don't use the summer one much any more."

"Why not?"

"Because I'm the only one left to use it. My wife is gone and my son lives too far away."

Brody went silent for a while, as if he needed a moment to absorb what I had said. Inside the gas station, Nicole was holding the receiver and looking grim.

Talking to Brody made me think about my own son, Scott. I wondered what time it was in California and whether he'd be in his apartment now or still at work. If I got to my place in time I was going to call and let him know about selling the summer house—where he had spent so many happy childhood days—so it wouldn't come as a surprise to him later. I'd been putting off the call for weeks, telling myself I was afraid he'd object and it would cause a further strain between us. But then last night I suddenly realized it was just the opposite: what I really feared is that he wouldn't care.

"What do you do?" Brody asked from over my shoulder. "For money?"

"I own an appliance store," I said. "At least I used to. I guess you could say I'm retired now."

"My mom's boyfriend is an artist," Brody said. "But sometimes he installs drywall."

"Here," I said. I reached around and worked the wet plastic bag over Brody's head. Underneath he had on a red down-filled hunting jacket just like his mother's, although his was tight and gaped between the buttons.

Just then I heard a knock on the glass behind my head. When I turned around I saw Nicole smiling in at me. Drops of sleet clung to her hair and eyebrows and lodged in the dimples on her cheeks.

"There's no answer at Celeste's," Nicole said. "I forgot she waitresses on Friday nights."

"Can't you call her at the restaurant where she works?"

"It's a new place. I don't remember the name." She twisted her mouth into an expression that was hard to interpret. "Besides, if you want to know the truth, she's actually a dancer. I don't think they let dancers take phone calls."

We stared at each other through the open window. In my mind a picture slowly formed: a smaller Nicole gyrating on the stage of some roadside bar, backlit by strobe lights, urged on by the whoops of deer hunters and drywall installers.

"Look," I said, "let's find some place to have a cup of coffee. We need to figure out what to do with you and Brody."

❄   ❄   ❄

We went to a restaurant called The Logging Camp, which was a favorite of Delores and mine in bygone days, and I treated Nicole and Brody to the Friday night perch dinner. The rough-cut plank walls were hung with paraphernalia of the lumber trade: crosscut saws and double-bladed axes, cant hooks, climbing spikes, sleds for hauling timber out of the woods. Next to our table a faded photograph of a lumber crew stared down on us, bearded men in heavy woolens and high-top leather boots, sober-faced and appearing to have a good deal on their minds. A hand notation in the corner said the year was 1887.

Ordinarily I don't like to be the center of attention but somehow Nicole got me to talking about myself. I told her about growing up during the Great Depression, and how I'd gotten married when I came back from Korea in '53. I told her about poor Delores, dead from cancer at sixty-four, and about Scott, who is a guide on one of the jungle cruise boats at Disneyland. I even told her about my store—Jimmy's Best-Buy Appliances, founded 1957—and how one of the national chains came into town last year and put me out of business. I suppose it all sounded pretty boring to Nicole, a woman who lived in sin with a welder-artist and got dumped along the highway. But I had to give her credit: she heard me out, nodded thoughtfully at all the right moments, made sympathetic murmurs here and there.

"That's too bad about your store," she said. Brody had taken a handful of my quarters and gone off to play Pac-Man in the lobby. "They oughtn't to allow chain stores," she added, "though that's only my uninformed opinion." She looked at me. "Why does your son want to live in California, anyway? All they've got out there is weirdoes."

"I think he likes the climate better," I said, although there was a lot more I could have added on that subject. I could have told her how things between me and Scott went downhill after Delores passed away and how he eventually decided the best solution was to put a continent between us. Like most kids these days Scott has a stubborn streak and tends to do whatever he pleases: like the year he spent living in an Idaho yurt, or his decision to leave law school to sign up on the jungle cruise. His attitude led to a lot of tension between us, and arguments that sometimes threatened to get out of hand. When Delores was around it was okay because she used her sweet disposition to calm the waters. She would urge me to keep quiet and to let Scott find his own way in life, even if it wasn't the way I would choose for him. Everyone has different needs, she said, and those needs change with the passing years, so what seems right to an older person might not be right for a younger one. I agreed with what she said, in principle, but I still could never keep from giving Scott my opinion. Even when it wasn't wanted.

Which was most of the time, of course.

"Well, at least you got to give him credit for being smart," Nicole said now.

"What?" I said.

Nicole gestured toward the window. Outside, the sleet was still coming down, making little ticking sounds as it struck against the glass.

"Oh, yes." I said. "You've got a point."

On the other side of the restaurant three men got up to leave. We watched in silence as they dropped some crumpled bills onto the center of their table, then clumped toward the door in heavy thermal boots. It was getting late. We were the only ones left in The Logging Camp.

"Listen," Nicole said. She leaned forward and placed her elbows on the table, then folded her hands like she was going to say a prayer. "I'm in a real spot here, mister. Celeste doesn't get off work 'til two. That's something I didn't tell you." She smiled guiltily and ducked her head like a child owning up to mischief. "Could you maybe let us stay at your place for the night? We've got nowhere else to go."

At first I didn't answer. The idea made sense—my house was only a few miles up the road now—but I liked Nicole and wanted her to find a better life. I thought I might turn the situation to her advantage by getting her to understand the fix she was in and how she had brought it on herself. She had reached this lonely moment on her own and facing it—feeling the pain of it—might do some good.

"I don't know if that'd be a good idea," I said in answer to her question.

"It'll be for just one night. By tomorrow Dwayne'll be looking for us. I'm sure of that. He's done this before and that's what always happens."

I stayed silent, staring at the plateful of fish bones in the center of the table. The incessant bong of Brody's Pac-Man drifted in from the lobby, sounding lonely and forlorn.

"I don't know, Nicole," I said for the second time, scratching my head. "I've got a lot of work to do up there and I can't be fussing with guests. It's not easy closing down a place for winter. You've got to drain the pipes, bring in the porch furniture, put antifreeze in all the sink drains."

Nicole stared at her folded hands, a frown pinching the corners of her eyes. She stared like that for a long time. When she finally looked up she wore a changed expression: her smile had hardened and she tossed her head in a coquettish way. She lifted a wayward strand of hair between two fingers and anchored it fetchingly behind one ear.

"Maybe I could make it worth your while," she said, using a voice that was barely above a whisper. She smiled in a wan, ingratiating way. "Maybe we could do a little snuggling. You look like someone who could use some snuggling."

I stared at her in disbelief. Here I was trying to guide her to a better path and now she was proposing to go further down the reckless road she was already traveling on. Some people are just beyond the reach of Christian kindness. Nicole, I guess, was one.

I cleared my throat. "I guess it'd be fine for you and Brody to spend the night, Nicole," I said quietly. "But that— what you're suggesting—is something I just couldn't do." I gave her a sharp look. "And I'm disappointed you'd make such an offer."

The moment turned awkward all the way around. Nicole peered into my face, trying to read my thoughts. I turned away and studied the lumber crew, rough men standing knee deep in virgin snow, somber as judges. Looking closer, I realized with a shock that behind their beards they were just kids; young men aiming to strike it rich in the lumber boom of northern Michigan.

Across the table Nicole emitted a tiny sniffle. I took out my handkerchief and handed it over. "Thanks," she said, touching it delicately to the corners of her eyes. "I'm sorry about asking you that. I guess I don't belong with decent people."

My eyes drifted back to the photograph. "Maybe it's time to make some changes, Nicole," I said. "You know, clean up your act. Stop living in sin with that Dwayne fellow. Get some training for a better job. Maybe slim down a little and begin to dress like a lady."

Nicole handed back my handkerchief, damp now with her tears. "I should probably just throw myself in front of a train," she said. "The world would be better off without me."

I knew Nicole deserved an answer. She had temporarily lost her hold on things and was reaching out a supplicating hand. But nothing came to mind, no words of comfort or wisdom or inspiration. Instead, I just kept looking into the faces of the logging crew, boys long dead now, every one.

❋   ❋   ❋

The sleet was coming down harder now, spotting the windshield with half-dollar-sized explosions. I cranked up the wipers to a faster speed; they screeched across the windshield, sounding like the cries of a wounded animal.

Nicole was turned around in her seat, playing word games with Brody—which was fine with me because I really didn't have anything more to say to her. After our conversation in the restaurant I knew we stood on opposite sides of a divide—of age and temperament and understanding—and there was no point trying to bridge it.

We passed through the village of Grand Marais—a couple of bars, a grocery store, a turn-of-the-century post office where a solitary light bulb reflected off a bank of safe deposit boxes—and then the road swung east and we ran along the shore of the lake. Black water stretched out to nowhere. Lights twinkled prettily across the bay. Through the mist of sleet I saw the slow incessant throb of the lighthouse beam on Whitefish Point.

I'd made this drive a thousand times and it always brought a welling in my chest, dislodging memories of the old days, trips north with Delores and Scott for happy summer holidays. Now Delores was dead and Scott was living on the other edge of the continent. But *my* life had still not changed. I inhabited the same big house, attended the same church every Sunday, went through the same steady motions of a comfortable, middling life. It's hard to alter the ingrained habits of a lifetime, I've found, and that includes my summer place: each spring I open it up and every fall I close it down, though in between no one is there.

I turned onto the gravel drive that led up to the house, a wood-framed bungalow sitting on a rocky rise above the water.

"Wait here," I said to Nicole. "I'll go in and turn on some lights."

Inside, the air was as chill and dank as a pharaoh's tomb and a thick coating of dust clung to everything. Dried-up insects littered the floor. A stiff dead mouse lay on the kitchen counter.

I found some cordwood and after a few tries I had a fire blazing in the big fieldstone hearth. When I turned around Nicole was standing in the doorway, holding Brody in her arms, who was asleep. Lit by the flickering firelight and dressed in their puffy down-filled jackets they looked like members of some pagan tribe, and for all I knew they were. Nicole's breath plumed into the frigid air, making a little cloud around her head.

"Nice place, " she said, looking around at the timbered ceiling, the picture window giving out onto Lake Superior, pine walls hung with nautical charts and family photos.

"My wife and I bought it just after we were married," I said. "Property up here was cheap back then."

"So where can I put Brody?" she asked. She staggered dramatically as if she were about to collapse under Brody's awful weight.

"Back there," I said, nodding in the direction of the

bedroom. "You might find some of Scott's old pajamas in the bureau."

I poured myself a scotch, then wandered around, drink in hand, examining the bric-a-brac of a lifetime of summers: clusters of sea shells that hadn't seen water for two decades, a telescope for spotting passing freighters, the sun-bleached skull of a raccoon, a *Newsweek* announcing Reagan's second term. I went over and stood before the picture window and peered out, trying to see the lakeshore in the meager throw of the inside light.

"Can I have one of those?" In the window's reflection I saw Nicole standing in the doorway. She wore one of Delores' old terrycloth bathrobes. Evidently she'd decided my invitation about the bedclothes applied to her as well as Brody.

I dropped a couple of ice cubes into a glass, splashed in some scotch and handed it over to Nicole. She took a good-sized swallow, holding the glass with both hands and watching me over the rim. Then she arranged herself at one end of the couch, drawing the bathrobe demurely around her legs.

I turned and faced the picture window that looked out toward Canada. I knew it was time to call Scott and tell him about my decision. But seeing all of this old stuff had put me in a mellow mood, and now I wasn't sure I could make that call. I seemed to be floating in a time warp where nothing much mattered, and maybe I'd been there for a while, and maybe for too long. After all, in the end we all end up like the hopeful boys standing in the snow at the logging camp.

Behind me I heard the gentle clink of ice cubes.

"Nicole," I said, still staring out the window. "I'm sorry about what I said to you in the restaurant. I don't have any business giving you advice about how to live your life. My own is far from perfect, if the truth were known."

In the fireplace a burning log collapsed, sending up a fury of sparks.

"What about the remark about losing weight?" Nicole said.

"I'm sorry about that, too. You're a fine looking woman. And you're a good mother to Brody. And I'd like nothing more than to take you up on your offer. Only I never knew any woman but Delores and it's too late for me to change now. But that doesn't have anything to do with this place; you and Brody can stay here for however long you want to."

For several long minutes there was only silence broken by the intermittent crack of fire logs and the lazy clink of ice cubes. My thoughts turned to Delores, who sat where Nicole was sitting not so many years ago, and I wondered what *she* would say if she could see me now. She had always been the peacemaker, the one who understood the blessed necessity of adapting and moving on, the one who struggled to bring me and Scott together, always managing to find some scrap of common ground where we could stand for a little while longer.

"So will you forgive me?" I asked Nicole.

"Forgive you for what?"

"For being an old curmudgeon, I guess?"

"What's a curmudgeon?"

I gave her question some thought before I answered. "Someone who's forgotten that life is just this moment," I said.

"Let me think about it," Nicole said. Then, after another long silence: "If we turn off the lights you can probably see the water better." I heard a pull chain rattle and the room went dark.

And then I did what Nicole suggested, and what Delores in her special wisdom would no doubt approve of too, strained to see beyond the void that lurked outside my window, to catch a glimpse of the shore in what was now the normal blackness of the night. At first everything was dark, but then my eyes adjusted and an image began to form—muted, indistinct, full of danger—the angry slant of sleet across the windowpane, the confused splash of waves against the rocky shore below, and in reflection—I think I had it right—someone rising from the sofa.

Bridge

It's not the landscape the old man imagined when he read the story last night in the thirty-five dollar Saint Ignace motel room. Because the story spoke of hills, both in the town of Seney and in the surrounding countryside, and of a steep uphill climb that made the hike from town so tiring for Nick and that caused him—a young man—to stop and nap.

Whereas now he sees that the land for five miles around is as flat as the proverbial pancake.

And the railroad bridge where Nick stood and looked down into the river after getting off the train is not what the old man had pictured either. Not a classic steel truss bridge but just two wooden timbers supporting ties and rails, with gaps between the ties where he can see the flowing water down below.

Nothing like the image that formed in his mind when he read the story last night.

Not to mention when he'd read it forty years ago.

But the town itself is close to what the author had described: a few wood-framed houses scattered across a barren scrubland; large open spaces where the saloons had once stood; the weed-choked foundation of an old hotel.

But the river bottom is sand, not stone and gravel, and the slack late-summer current does not "swell smooth" against the bridge pilings, and no trout are observed to be holding in the current, much less moving "at quick angles."

So the story is a combination of truth and falsehoods after all.

Not a thing you can rely on.

This is what he knows from having read about it:

On a late August day in 1919 the author (then twenty and not yet an author) and two of his friends rode a train from Petoskey to Mackinaw City, some fifty miles north, where they transferred to a railroad ferry that took them across the Straits of Mackinac into Michigan's upper peninsula. In the town of Saint Ignace they re-boarded the train and rode for another seventy miles to Seney, a logging boomtown that had flourished during the 1880s and '90s but was by then largely abandoned. The young men spent the next week camping in the area north of Seney and fishing the waters of the Fox River, both the main branch and the much smaller east branch.

Some five years later, when the author was living in Paris with his new wife, he used Seney and the area around it as the setting for a short story. For "poetic reasons" he took the name of another Michigan river, the Two-Hearted River, and used it in the title of his story. The story was unusual; nothing like it had been written before. It had only one character, no dialogue, and no plot. It told vaguely of a young man named Nick Adams who uses the pleasures and rituals of fishing and camping to deal with some great internal strife. The source of the strife is never explained, though somehow the reader comes to understand that it had something to do with a recent experience in war. The story ends with the young man turning back from a particularly tangled stretch of river because he doesn't feel up to fishing in such difficult waters.

In 1925 the story was published in an obscure volume along with other stories by the author. It was the final story, and thus, presumably, the most emblematic of whatever the author was trying to say. Over the ensuing years it was praised for its stylistic innovation, its ability to convey much more than was stated, and its relentless realism. It's not an exaggeration to say that it's become one of the most famous short stories in the English language.

❄   ❄   ❄

It's a trip the old man had planned to make for several years but kept putting off, possibly because he didn't know *why* he wanted to make it, and a 360-mile drive from Detroit and two lost days of work didn't seem worth it. Or possibly from the fear of surrendering to a part of himself he had reliably suppressed for most of four decades (the part—if he were honest about it—that he had once considered best).

He had seen the author's boyhood home, his first Paris apartment, a later Paris apartment where he'd composed a famous novel, and the Idaho house where he had died. None of these visits, though, was premeditated in the way this trip has been; they were last-minute excursions added on to other travels, impetuous efforts to reclaim something he had left behind. Still, having sought out those places—even in a non-purposeful way—suggests a tendency toward obsession that he finds a little embarrassing in a man his age. In the same category as standing at a stage door to glimpse a famous actress, or interrupting a celebrity's dinner to ask for an autograph.

And so he thinks back over the last few weeks, looking for some reason that might explain this impulse to head north *now*. But nothing comes to mind. His life these last few days and weeks has been uneventful, a normal collection of minor tribulations: a spousal disagreement, a slight professional setback, the disconcerting results of a blood test. Nothing like the soul-wrenching strife felt by young Nick.

❄   ❄   ❄

He drives a short distance out into the countryside and pulls off onto the shoulder of the road. Using a small spiral notebook he tallies up the score so far:

THINGS THAT WERE TRUE

The town. More or less as described.

The road going north that Nick hiked on (although, as noted, it does not rise).

An abundance of ferns in the surrounding countryside.

A general preponderance of conifers (Jack pine and white pine especially).

Grasshoppers arcing out of the grassy meadows. Exactly as described.

Burned stumps from some long-ago forest fire, suggestive of widespread devastation.

THINGS THAT WERE UNTRUE

The aforementioned railroad bridge.

No hills!

The river flows are slack in late summer.

The river bottom is sand and clay, not pebbles and boulders (as previously noted).

No "islands of pine trees" were observed (not to mention the higher ground needed to see them from).

So the story was a mingling of truth and falsehoods after all. A clever subterfuge. And this, he understands now, is the real reason he's come north these many miles—to understand once and for all that the real world does not conform to the one he's carried in his imagination for so long. And to thereby gain a kind of validation for the course he chose to follow. A course that rejected imagination in favor of facts and hard realities.

Where was the author honest and where was he making it up?

Or—put another way—what blend of fact and artifice was made to feel like truth?

And it's possible, he suddenly realizes, that truth has become more important to him in these later years. After all, he's closing in on life's last great adventure, approaching the age where the mix of fact and artifice no longer worked for the man who was the boy who went on that memorable fishing trip so long ago. And he (evidently) has some of the same burdens in tow.

He looks out over the countryside; after a moment he slips the car into gear and begins to move ahead.

North of town along an unnamed gravel road he sees the main branch of the river that Nick camped beside and fished in on that fictional morning. The river where he caught two trout and seemed to be in control of things for a while.

He stops to make a closer examination, noting the features of the river and surrounding countryside, like a scientist seeking clues to support some radical hypothesis. The river is not wide here, only about thirty feet across, but it's deep and moves along at a lively pace. It's a pretty river, snaking its way through the shallow tilt of forest landscape, its silvery surface alive with eddies and ripples and swirls. But he notes again that the soil is heavy and clay-like, and he knows that it must certainly make for difficult fishing. Nevertheless, he walks back to the car and puts on his rubber waders, assembles his casting rod, makes his ungainly way back to the river and shuffles down the slippery bank. But as soon as he steps out into the current his fears are confirmed: not only is the water deep but his feet sink several inches into the clay bottom. With each step he has to thrust forward in a way that threatens to tip him off balance. After a few awkward casts he gives up and returns to the car.

His thoughts while reclining in a sunny meadow after an abortive fishing adventure:

When was the first time you read it? A bright spring day in the rented house in Ann Arbor. Your last year of college when you were trying to decide between a fishing boat in Canada and the factory where they built the Chevrolets.

And how many times have you read it since? Five or six. Maybe more. (Not including the preparation for this trip, which was research and therefore shouldn't be counted.)

And what do you think you got out of it? Hard to say. A sense of how life feels, perhaps. A lesson in how to confront difficulties. Which is to say a lesson in toughness, pleasant distractions, and, finally, graceful surrender.

Which you've had to use a few times in your life.

And no doubt will again.

The author was not the first to touch you but he was the first to show that art could be derived from a world you recognized. Art could have muscle and sinew and speak of hard, uncomfortable truths. It could be expressed in simple language, carefully chosen. And it could take as its inspiration nothing more significant than a fishing trip to Seney, Michigan.

In other words, he was the first to give you a different way of looking at the world.

He's ready to head back home but he has one more stop to make: the stretch of river that caused Nick to lose heart and return to camp. The "bad-hearted" river, if you will. That's the story's final revelation: that last piercing look into Nick's troubled soul. The moment of dignified surrender that the whole story leads to.

He consults a map and sees that the east branch of the Fox runs roughly north and east of town, so he drives out on the county highway and takes a turn-off that seems to head in the right direction. After a mile the bumpy two-track ends abruptly in a field of ferns and fire-scarred stumps.

He parks and continues along on foot, enters a thick forest, keeping the sun ahead and to the right. And then through the shadowed underbrush he sees the glint of flowing water, a dark moving slab punctuated by shafts of sunlight. When he reaches the bank he sees it's not much more than a stream, just eight or ten feet wide. It's not the swamp described in the story but it has the other attributes noted: high slippery banks, overhanging branches, roots and snags along the bottom, thick water grasses undulating in the current, rotting trees. It's not the swamp of the story but it's a pretty good substitute. A place you wouldn't want to fish in, even if big fish beckoned.

He gazes at the small course of water winding its way across the forest bottom, not really sure what he should do next. At some level he realizes this moment is the culmination of his journey, the replication of a fictional event that presumed to offer some insight into the human condition, and that has evidently weighed down on his own life with some force, too. He'd like to take something back, some revelation small or large, some penetrating insight. Some truth. But he's not sure what he feels. Or what he wants to feel. Or what he should feel.

So he stands there trying to force the experience to some conclusion, but after several minutes of silent staring the only thought that comes to mind is that he's all alone here in the forest. At considerable effort and for motives that are unclear—and possibly foolish—he's brought himself into a dark, uncomfortable place that not too many people know about, or would care to visit, even if they did. And standing in this particular place on this particular July afternoon—trying to discover the *actual* or the *want* or the *should* of the experience—means finally nothing at all.

Nothing without the imagination the author brought to it.

He considers this for a moment, then turns away.

Two hours later he's approaching the giant suspension bridge that spans the five-mile gap between Lakes Michigan and Huron. He feels a nagging foolishness, a slight regret for having wasted so much time. Already his mind is casting ahead to the challenges waiting back home: the spousal disagreement (probably resolvable with a little humility); the minor professional setback (calling for diplomacy and hard work); the unwelcome results of the blood test (a possible prelude to some sinister decline, though statistics, he has been told, are on his side).

He comes up onto the deck of the bridge and begins the long easy climb to the center. An opening occurs in the traffic and he steers over into the slower lane, thinking he'd like to prolong the experience of crossing this magnificent structure. Cars dart in and out around him. A semi rumbles past. A horn blasts. Wind, notching through the narrow joining of waters, buffets the car.

At last he reaches the summit and begins the slow descent. In front, green hills rise up along the far shore, which is to say the northernmost tip of the giant peninsula that has been his home for more than sixty years. The stage on which his life has played out, he muses, and on which a few new chapters can hopefully still be written.

He has never trusted invention—he understands this now more than ever—though he *has* stubbornly believed that truth can sometimes swell against the cold quick slide of life and a kind of comprehension can follow. And then this thought occurs to him, and it's the thought he will remember when he thinks about this trip in later years: that this crossing marks the real end of his journey, and that a trip that began with the image of a fictional bridge is ending with the crossing of a real one.

Fact and artifice—and something that feels like truth.

A warm July afternoon and he's returning home.